TAK

**The Coldest Fae
Book One**

By Katerina Martinez

Gwendolyn Elizabeth Sommers - Hill 2021 year 7/7X

# TAKEN (THE COLDEST FAE, BOOK 1)

Chapter One

Madame Lydia Whitmore took her sweet arse time coming out of the changing room, leaving me to wonder if she'd forgotten I was even here. It had been twenty minutes since I'd handed her the dress I'd made; twenty minutes since the last time I'd seen another person.

And I really needed to pee.

Don't get me wrong, you could fit my entire house in the room I'd been left in. A vaulted ceiling made the room appear tall, its white walls gave it incredible depth, and the gorgeous hardwood floors told the story of the many dancing troupes that had danced upon it over the decades.

I was happy with the visuals. But really, I just wanted to get paid, use the bathroom, and be on my way.

"There's a bathroom down the hall, Dahlia," came a tiny voice near my ear.

"What are you doing out?" I hissed, trying not to make any sudden movements. The last thing I wanted was for Lydia to know I had a pixie with me. Humans weren't supposed to have magical pets, and mages like her were sticklers for enforcing those kinds of rules. But Gullie was more than a pet; she was my only friend.

And if I ever called her a pet, I was likely to get smacked around the mouth for it.

"I got bored waiting in your hair," Gullie said, her little wings buzzing against my ear. I watched her zip around in front of me, her tiny, glowing body leaving a light, glittering trail of fairy dust in the air wherever she went.

"Please get back inside?" I pleaded, "You know what'll happen if they catch you."

Gullie stared at me and folded her arms. Her translucent, butterfly wings were impossible to see when she was flying, but the scowl on her pretty little face was as clear as day. "Do you really expect me to stay in your hair the whole time we're out?"

"That was the deal, remember?"

"Do you have any idea what it's like being stuck in your hair all day?"

My eyes widened and I sucked in a breath. "What's wrong with my hair? I'm clean. I use conditioner."

"Yeah, and by the way, that doesn't make my job of holding on any easier." She cocked a thumb behind her back. "I have wings. I can fly. But instead I have to hold onto silky smooth strands of hair to keep from toppling out."

"Look, they aren't just my rules, okay? I just… I don't want anyone taking you away from me."

Gullie frowned, then sighed. "Don't do that…" she said, hovering closer to my face. It was easier to see her the closer she got to me. Her body radiated this bright green glow if you saw her from a distance, but the glow fell away up close. She looked like me, almost, if I was the size of the palm of my own hand and had shocking green hair. "You know I wouldn't let anyone pull us apart," she said.

"I know. I think I'm just uncomfortable, here. Mages make me feel weird."

"It's because they're classist arseholes. Just picture them all naked, it makes it easier to deal with them."

A door started to open, and Gullie zipped back into my hair. I swatted at the trail of shimmering pixie dust she'd left in the air, then abruptly stood to try and mask my sudden flailing. Lydia's assistant came through the door first; a severe looking woman with a black bob and a pencil dress that wasn't terribly flattering to her figure.

She stopped and stared at me for a long moment, one hand grabbing onto the door she'd just opened, her eyes narrow. After a short while, she pulled the door open the rest of the way and stepped aside, allowing Lydia to step through into the studio.

I'd only ever met this woman a handful of times, but she'd never looked quite as radiant as she did now. She was statuesque, a giraffe in human form with long, golden locks of hair, striking, pointed features, and all the grace of a princess.

The gown she was wearing shimmered as she moved. It was low cut in the front and back, and pearlescent, catching the sunlight and reflecting every color of the rainbow in wonderful, rippling waves.

My heart surged into a quick beat.

I'd made that dress with my own two hands. It was one thing to see it on a mannequin in my dull little workshop, and quite another to watch it come to life on the body of a woman beautiful enough to do it justice. Then I caught myself in the long mirror running along the entire length of one wall, and I frowned.

I was short and pale, my hair a dull, uninspiring kind of brown, my body slight and petite. A black beanie hat sat on my head, I was wearing my lucky blue scarf and black sweater over a floaty skirt. I only wore a little makeup, enough to darken my eyes and bring a little contrast to my otherwise pasty complexion.

In other words, princess, meet peasant.

The only thing we had in common was, we were both wearing clothes I had made myself.

"Wow..." I gaped, staring at Lydia as she glided across the room toward the mirror.

She spun around once, twice, three times. Each time she did, the dress would shimmer and move with her form like it was made of water. She was radiant, immaculate, and yet, she made a sound I wasn't expecting to hear.

"Hmmm."

I stared at her. *Hmmm?* What did *hmmm* mean? Didn't she like it? Not to blow my own trumpet, but the dress was my finest work yet. I'd never made anything quite so perfect before and wasn't sure if I'd be able to do so again, not for a while. Working with real, magic, Night Spinner thread wasn't easy, but the payment from this dress was going to solve so many problems, the many weeks of frustration and insane tiredness would be worth it in the end.

But she's said hmmm.

"It's stunning," I said, deciding to finally speak. "I mean, you're glowing right now."

"It is quite spectacular," Lydia said, her voice delicate, but firm; the voice of a graceful disciplinarian. "But…"

"Is… there something wrong?" I ventured, my heart racing now for a different reason. "Is it the fit? Because I can adjust it."

"No, the fit is fine. The dress itself is fine." Lydia twirled again, her blonde curls cascading gently over her shoulders. "There's just… I'm not sure. I feel like something's missing. Is something missing, Dawn?"

Fine? I would've been seething if I wasn't on the verge of a panic attack.

"I think you look regal," Dawn said, "The Queen herself has never worn a dress quite like this one before."

Good. That's good. More of that, please.

"I don't know," Lydia said. "I like it, but I'm not in love with it."

"Whatever it is, I can fix it," I said, taking a step toward her only to instantly regret it.

Lydia snapped around to glare at me, her nostrils flared, her lips curled into a frown. Meekly, I took a step back, remembering my place. I was human, she was a mage. Mother Helen had taught me better than to step toward another mage like that. They didn't like humans getting so *familiar*.

I'd just made the situation ten times worse. Great.

For some strange reason, Lydia decided to soften up a little instead of zapping me to death. She stared at me from atop her turned up nose and lazy eyes, almost like she was sizing me up. "I want a discount," she said.

And there it was, the real reason for this show she was putting on. It wasn't that she didn't like the dress. The dress was perfect. Christ, it was *magic*. What she wanted was to pay less than we'd agreed, and that meant she wasn't just a snobby bitch; she was a cheap one, too.

"A... discount?" I asked, "But, we already agreed on the price."

"And you have been paid half of what we'd originally agreed," she said, "However, you haven't entirely delivered on your part of the transaction, though, have you?"

"I haven't?"

She turned to the mirror again. "You promised this dress would make me younger."

"No, I said the dress would make you look and feel younger. I also promised it wouldn't lose its shimmer for over a hundred years, I promised the seams would never break, and I promised it would be hand-stitched to fit your exact shape. I've made good on all of those promises, so far, so I don't understand why you want to pay less?"

"You forget yourself, *girl*," Dawn barked. She was sneering at me from the door, like a Pitbull guarding its owner. "You are addressing Madame Lydia Whitmore, Mistress of the Whitmore Academy of Ballet, and you will address her with the respect she deserves."

I glared at the heavyset woman by the door. "I'm not being disrespectful, but I don't think it's right to change the terms of a deal." I turned to face Lydia again. "With all due respect, I spent weeks making this dress for you. My family is grateful for your business, but I didn't come here to haggle over a price that had already been agreed upon. I don't think you're the kind of person to go back on your word, are you?"

Lydia cocked a quizzical eyebrow… and then promptly kicked me out of her academy. Dawn, the *Pitbull*, escorted me downstairs and practically shoved me into the cold, wet London street. Honestly, I was lucky to have walked out of that place with even the twenty percent of what Madame Whitmore owed me in my hand.

I'd pushed the limits of what she would take from a *human*, and I'd blown it. Mother Helen was going to be furious. We needed the money the dress was going to bring in, we were counting on it, and I was coming back home with only a fraction of it.

I slid the envelope with the money in it into my backpack as I walked and zipped it shut. I wanted to get back home quick, thinking maybe if I got home fast enough, Mother Helen could sort this mess out.

I was so in my own head, so eager to rush home, I didn't notice the guy I'd bumped into until I was already halfway to the floor.

My backpack went one way, and I went another. I was lucky I'd shut it, otherwise its contents would've spilled all over the sidewalk. I, however, wasn't so lucky. I went down hard, falling arse-first into a puddle because, of course, there were puddles everywhere.

I was about to get up and apologize for running into the guy, when someone walking past my backpack kicked it into the road — maybe absentmindedly, maybe on purpose. This was London. It was hard to tell.

I scrambled toward it on all fours and stretched for it, managing to barely grab and pull it out of the path of a black cab that came rushing by. But the cab rolled over a dip in the road as it trundled by, a dip filled with water.

I was instantly soaked, from my head to my toes.

"*Fantastic*," I sighed, clutching the backpack to my chest, water dripping down my face.

Then a hand appeared next to my head. I took it, not really thinking about who the hand belonged to before taking it and got myself back on my feet. When I turned around, I found myself staring into the eyes of an angel in a fitted suit.

He was easily the most beautiful, most intense looking man I had ever laid eyes on. His hair was as black as the night, slicked back around the front but pulled into a bun at the back and long at the sides. His beard, his lips, his eyebrows; everything about his face screamed *brute strength*, except for his eyes. His eyes were gray and sharp, and sparkled with a kind of cold, cunning intelligence that made my heart hammer inside of my chest.

Those same eyes narrowed and fixed on mine.

I returned the stare, becoming instantly aware that I probably looked like a drowned rat. I also realized I hadn't yet let go of his hand. I tried to pull away, but his grip on it tightened and, in fact, he started pulling me toward *him*.

"Excuse me—" I started to say, but he plunged his nose into my hair before I could get the words out.

Breathless I stood as this man took a deep whiff of my hair, then abruptly pulled away, a look of stunned shock in those crystalline eyes.

"*Belore…*" he said, the word spilling from his lips on the back of a sigh.

My skin prickled. "What did you say?" I asked, even as my breath caught in my throat.

I'd never been *sniffed* like that before. Part of me was desperate to get the hell away from him, but another part was still tingling all over. I didn't know what the hell was going on. But something was happening to me. It was as if, deep inside of me, something was waking up; something ancient and primal, something *written*.

Belore.

I felt his grip slacken, and I took the opportunity to yank my arm away from him and start backing off. "Thanks for helping me up," I called out, and heading directly for the nearest London Underground station as quickly as I could.

He simply gawked at me, confusion written all over his face—his *perfect* face.

I got a chance to take one last look at him before entering the Underground, before the masses of tourists and Londoners alike became too thick that we wouldn't be able to see each other. I didn't think I'd ever forget him, or the way his suit so tightly clung to what I suspected was one hell of a body.

Who the hell was he? Some kind of high-powered executive, probably. He probably drove a Bentley, or a Mercedes. One thing was for sure, he wouldn't have given me a second look if I hadn't literally smashed into him on the street.

I moved into the Underground station, losing sight of him completely. It was time to go home and face the music, face reality, face my *mothers*.

Chapter Two

I didn't have one mother—I had three.
Mother Pepper.
Mother Evie.
And, of course, Mother Helen.

They weren't my biological mothers. I wasn't grown in a tube, but I *had* been adopted. My real parents were gone. Not dead, necessarily. Just gone. I didn't know who my real parents were, or how I came to fall into the laps of the three caring, amazing women who raised me.

To be honest, I didn't need to know anything else. They had given me the life I had. The only life I could ever have wanted. I owed everything to them, and that was why coming home with my tail between my legs stung as bad as it did. I felt like I'd failed them.

My mothers owned and operated a haberdashery in Carnaby Street, in London. For the everyday human, we sold the fabrics, the tools, and all the other knickknacks a person looking to make their own outfits would ever need.

Everyone who walked through our doors was made to feel welcomed, and like they'd made the right choice in deciding to wear the things they could make instead of buying the kinds of mass-produced, massively overpriced, low quality clothes you'd find at a shop.

Of course, there was more to the shop than that.

Ask the right questions, and the door to the backroom opens. In there, you might just find anything from enchanted threads, to potions, to little oddities useful to those with a flair for *magic*. See, my mothers were all mages, and even though that made me—the human—kind of an oddball at home, it also meant I should've known better when dealing with Lydia.

Sorry, Madame Arsehole Whitmore.

"I need to talk to you," Gullie said into my ear as I walked beneath the arching, brightly lit and multi-colored sign that opened Carnaby Street. *The Magic Box* sat tucked away at the end of an alley not far from the entrance. It was a little out of sight, but that was fine. We didn't make our business on foot traffic.

"Not now," I hissed.

"No, it's important."

"Look, I'm about to walk into a hornet's nest. Unless what you've got to tell me is life-or-death, it can wait. Is it life or death?"

"It could be."

"Okay, Mother Helen is definitely going to kill me, so this takes priority. Besides, you've had this whole trip to talk to me."

"You don't like me talking to you while there's humans around. Are there any humans around now?"

"You make a good point, but still, *no*."

The Magic Box itself barely looked like a shop at all. It was a ruddy brown building at the end of a deep alleyway with a single black door and a little window looking onto the cobblestone street outside. I opened the door without knocking and stepped through. A bell jingled, and right away I was hit with the warm, inviting scent of freshly baked pastries.

Yes, that was probably a strange smell to come out of a haberdashery, but *strange* was our brand.

Stacks upon stacks of rolled up fabrics lined two of the shop's walls. Walking through it, there were aisles covered in tools, bits, bobs, and even more fabrics to look through. In here, you'd find everything you could possibly need, whether you wanted to make a modern looking summer dress, or a classic, turn of the century, historically accurate, ballgown.

Mother Pepper was stationed behind the desk at the far end of the room. She perked up at the sound of the bell, then smiled when she saw me. She was a jolly woman, fairly ample herself, and getting on in years, but she had a kind, grandmotherly spirit and she loved to cook. I'd barely arrived at the desk, and already she held a small pastry in her hand for me to take a bite out of. The light fell out of her kind eyes when she saw the state of me.

"Oh, darling, you're soaked," she said, "What happened?"

I grabbed the pastry, stuffed it into my mouth, and started chewing. It was delicious. I was getting cinnamon, apple, cream; all the ingredients in an apple pie. But there was something else, too. Something I couldn't put my finger on, but it turned the taste up to eleven. "Oh, that's really good," I said, "Apple pie, right?"

Mother Pepper stared at me from behind her half-moon spectacles. "It's not apple. It's something called a Lerac fruit. It's exceedingly rare, only the Goblins know how to find it. I bought some this morning."

"Tastes a bit like apple."

"A bit, yes, if you prepare it the way I have. But unlike an apple, a Lerac fruit will sharpen your senses for a time. She pulled a handkerchief out from under the desk and handed it to me. "Now, care to tell me why you're drenched?"

I shrugged. "Not really… is Mother Helen around?"

"Yes, she's in the back." Mother Pepper paused. "You did hand the dress over to Madame Whitmore, yes?"

"Yes mother, I did."

Mother Pepper lit up and rapidly clapped her hands, making the bangles on her wrist jingle. "Oh, splendid!" she said, "I take it she liked the dress?"

"Yeah… I should go and talk to Mother Helen."

"Is everything alright, child?" she lightly touched my face with the back of her hand, "You're looking a little pale."

I shook my head. "I'm always pale."

"Paler than usual, then. Are you sure you're alright?"

"Yeah, I'm fine." I picked up another pastry and ate it as I walked through the beaded curtain and into the back.

The corridors in our shop were tight and dark, barely wide enough for one person to walk without their shoulders touching the walls. A set of stairs to the right led the way up to our house, which sat on top of the store. Going straight ahead and through the door at the end of the corridor, though, took you to *the back*; a codename for our little magic shop.

I found the door slightly ajar as I reached it, a shaft of light breaking from the other side. I pushed the door open and moved through, swallowing the last of my apple—*Lerac?*—pie as I reached the magic shop. The space in here wasn't much bigger than the space out front, but it looked it thanks to the lack of fabric stacks all over the place.

In here, there were shelves, and tables, and cupboards all filled with many wonderful, strange, and increasingly random things. From crystals with bits of magic in them, to strange books, to needles of all shapes and sizes, and spindles of thread that shimmered with the light. There were also potions all throughout, whole racks of bottles filled with liquids of all colors, some of which bubbled or faintly glowed.

Mother Helen wasn't back here, but Mother Evie was. She sprang up from her workstation and squealed, her long, black hair bouncing as she bounded toward me like a speeding train. "You're *back*!" she said, throwing her arms around me and scooping me up. Mother Evie was the youngest of the three, she could've been my older sister. Her eyes were so wide and bright; childlike, almost, and sparkling with magic. "Your first delivery! How did it go?"

Ah. Yes. This had been the first time my mothers had entrusted *me* to go and deliver a dress to one of our clients. Because that only made things better.

"Ummmm…" I said, trailing off. "As well as it could've gone, given the circumstances?"

She pulled away and bopped me on the nose with her finger. "Well, *that* doesn't sound terribly good, does it? Come, you must tell me *all* about it."

I didn't have a choice. Mother Evie dragged me across to her workbench and sat me down on the stool she'd been sitting on. She was a seamstress, too. Her desk was covered in rolls of fabric, scissors, and needles. We didn't use machines, here. Everything was hand-sewn. Mostly because the kinds of clothes we made had the tendency of making man-made machine we put them through… explode.

I'd learned *that* the hard way.

"So?" Mother Evie asked, "What happened?"

I shook my head. "It didn't go great."

"No?"

"No. It really didn't. I think I really messed it up."

She cocked her head to the side. "No, don't say that. How could you possibly have messed it up?"

"She… said something was missing. I don't think she liked it."

One of her hands flew to her mouth. "Oh, no."

"I don't know why. She kept saying it wasn't right, but it was. I spent ages working on it. It was perfect."

"I'm so sorry, sweetie. That sounds awful." She scoffed. "That woman doesn't know *what* she's talking about. I'm sure she'll come around."

"I don't know if she will. I felt like she just didn't want to pay what we'd agreed to pay."

"What would make you think that?"

"Because she *didn't* pay what had been agreed," came a stern, older voice from the other side of the room. *Mother Helen.* "Did she?"

I swallowed my nerves and shook my head. "No."

"And you left without making her keep her end of the deal… didn't you?"

"I didn't know what else to do, I—"

Mother Helen waved her hand, a gesture that usually meant *keep the hell quiet*. "Come with me. Now." With that, she disappeared into an adjoining room.

"I'm in trouble," I said.

Mother Evie squeezed my shoulder and smiled. "Go," she whispered, "It'll be alright. It's not like she's going to turn you into a frog, or anything… not after the last time."

"Don't remind me. I get nightmares every time I think about it."

I took a deep breath and rose to my feet, then I followed Mother Helen into *my* little workroom feeling only a *little* more optimistic after what Mother Evie had said. She was right. I wasn't going to get turned into a toad again, but there were plenty more animal shapes I could be made into as punishment.

Chapter Three

Of my mothers, Mother Helen was the disciplinarian. She was like every single school headmistress I'd ever crossed paths with, only about ten times scarier and gifted with magic. Mother Helen was tall, probably as tall as Madame Whitmore, and possessed of the same kind of grace, although hers was more refined and less entitled, like an aged wine, and suited to her incredible intelligence and poise. She was also one hell of a dresser, looking as she did with her choice of black dresses and corsets, like she belonged in the Victorian age.

I didn't speak as I walked through my workroom and found my stool to sit on. It was tiny, and a little cramped in here, but thanks to Mother Helen's insistence that I treat my place of work like a temple, the place was also immaculately kept. My rolls of fabric all had homes, the dress forms I used sat quietly in the corner, and my basic sewing supplies were properly organized, and never out of reach.

Not the magic stuff, though; that *was* kept out of my reach, and with good reason.

"Care to explain to me exactly how this happened?" Mother Helen asked, breaking through the silence like she had a sledgehammer.

"How do you *know* what happened?" I asked, trying my best not to sound too argumentative.

"I could sense your thoughts the moment you walked through the doors. You truly do wear your worries on your sleeve."

"I'm sorry. I didn't mean to screw it up, Madame Whitmore just—"

"—the Whitmores are a notoriously pompous, vainglorious lot who would sooner die than be seen in a sub-par outfit."

Anger flushed into my chest. "My dress wasn't sub-par."

"I know it wasn't. I also happen to know that family is cheap and will do anything they can to squander their wealth."

"Why did we do business with them?"

"Because we need it, child. I thought, perhaps, she would fall in love with the dress and not cause any trouble. Evidently, I was wrong, and I apologize."

"Wait... you're apologizing to *me*?"

"I should not have sent you to deliver the dress. I should've gone myself. Perhaps, then..."

"Why didn't you?"

Mother Helen's face hardened, her jade eyes bearing down on mine. "Because you are a Crowe, just like the rest of us. This family isn't a family without you, Dahlia, but I grow weary of having to put up with the disrespect our family gets."

I lowered my head. "Because of me, right? Because I'm human."

"No, child… because you have a gift they do not have. Because you are *better* than them."

I looked up at her again. "Better than them?" I scoffed. "Hardly. I can't do magic."

"Perhaps not, but your skill with a needle and thread are unmatched. You can work with the kind of silks not even your mothers can, not without either grave peril or great exhaustion."

I stared at her, trying not to frown. She was lying to me. Sure, what she was saying about my ability to fashion a dress out of strange, magical materials was true. I was good at that. But the other part, about me being human and that leading other mages to look down on our family? That was also true, and we both knew it.

It was also the reason why we were going out of business.

Six months ago, the Magic Box was flourishing. Our clothes were red hot, fresh orders coming in every single day. Mages wore our dresses to all sorts of events—none of which I'd ever been invited to, but I'd heard about them. The Solstice Ball, the Midsummer Ball, the New Year's Ball.

All the Balls.

Mages threw a lot of Balls.

Then Mother Helen had the idea of revealing to the world that, not only had their trio become a quartet — the magical community as a whole didn't know I even existed — but that I, a human, was the one responsible for crafting the *special-order* clothes mages came to buy from us.

That had been a mistake.

Maybe if she had talked to me about it, I may have been able to persuade her otherwise. I liked my life before. I still liked my life. But I hated the idea that anyone out there thought any less of the three wonderful women who had chosen to raise me as one of their own, even though they didn't have to.

I loved them, and they loved me; the instinct to protect each other was mutual, and I felt powerless — like the weak link in the chain.

"Let me go back to her," I said, "I mean, let me clean up first, and then let me go back. Maybe I can talk to her, and—"

"Absolutely not," Mother Helen said, shutting her eyes and shaking her head. "We aren't doing business with that family anymore, not if they are going to go back on their word. We may be simple seamstresses to them, but we should be proud enough to know our worth."

"I hear what you're saying, I really do… but I feel like I can get through to her. I know she loved the dress."

"I know. Pepper, Evie and I will be leaving immediately for the Whitmore Academy to collect the rest of our payment. For now, you are to stay here."

"Because I've done enough damage?"

Mother Helen approached and laid a gentle hand on my shoulder. "Sweet girl, no. Heavens, no. I am sure you were as polite and as courteous as I have taught you to be. You have done no damage, here. I would simply feel a lot more comfortable knowing you're here, safe at home… and *bathed*."

I remembered how ratty I probably looked. "Oh, yeah… long story."

A playful smirk. "Yes… *I know*."

My cheeks flushed bright red. Awkwardly, I shot to my feet, knocking over the stool I'd been sitting on. "Okay, well… I should go bathe," I said, and I slid past Mother Helen and made my way up to my bedroom.

Like my workroom, my bedroom was tiny, but roomy enough for me. A single bed sat pressed up against a corner, just beneath a window looking over the Magic Box's front door and the street beyond it. Against one of the far walls was my desk, mostly empty save for my laptop and a small desk organizer in which I kept the pens and pencils I used to design new clothes.

The thing that took up the most space was my wardrobe. That was filled with clothes I'd made myself, from jumpers, to blouses, to jeans, to dresses and everything in between. When I went out shopping, I didn't look for actual outfits, I bought fabric with which to make my own. I didn't wear anything I hadn't made myself. Not only did that save money, but it was also nice to wear stuff that fit me just right.

Gullie's wings fluttered against my ear as soon as I found myself alone, startling me. I wasn't used to the buzzing from her wings being so loud, but then I remembered what Mother Pepper had said about the pastries I'd just eaten.

Lerac fruits really did work.

The glowing green pixie shot out of my hair, zipped around my face, and *slapped* me across the cheek. It was the weirdest thing, getting slapped by a pixie. They looked like miniature humans with wings. You'd think getting slapped by one of them would feel like having a toothpick flicked at you. But with the help of a little magic, they could slap like a full-grown adult, and it *stung*.

"What the hell was that for?" I gasped, my hand flying to cover my face.

"That's for letting me get *soaked* earlier," Gullie said, "I never got to properly thank you. Now, if I could kindly have a moment of *her highness'* time, I have something important to tell you."

"Can it wait until after I have a shower? I'm pretty sure I look like crap and everyone's just too polite to tell me."

"No, it can't wait. It's about *him*."

"Him?" I cocked my head to the side. Then realization dawned. "Oh... *him*."

I remembered what had happened between us with vivid clarity. There wasn't a single detail that had escaped. Not the strength of his grip, not the shape of his body, nor the way I had felt when he pulled me in close and smelled my hair. It had been dripping at that point, and it probably smelled like rubber, tarmac, and who knew what else. But that didn't seem to have mattered to him.

Belore.

That's what he'd said to me. The one word he'd uttered—or growled, more like.

There was something *animal* about him, something primal. I remembered watching a video once of a wolf stalking a deer. The deer stood almost motionless in the wilderness, except for its chest. It must have been taking three breaths a second, paralyzed by fear having sensed a deadly predator had gotten hold of its scent.

Was that what he'd been doing? Had he been finding my scent? Whatever his intentions, I could now relate to that deer. I now knew what it felt like to feel my own heart start running away, to have my breathing suddenly shorten to an almost dangerous degree. The worst part? I'd liked it. *Jesus*, I'd liked the way that had felt.

I liked him, the way he looked, the shape of his face, his body. Never mind that he was probably just like that wolf; dangerous as fu—Gullie clicked her fingers in front of me, snapping me out of my thoughts. "Hello," she said, drawing the word out.

I shook my head. "What?" I asked, grabbing a fresh outfit from the wardrobe and starting to change out of my damp clothes.

"I lost you for a second, and I really can't lose you. Not right now. You need to listen to me."

"Alright, I'm listening."

Gullie buzzed a little closer to me. "You need to be careful," she said. "That man, I don't know who he was, but he was fae."

A wave of cold and hot rushed through me. "*Fae?*" I asked, my voice rising a little too high.

The little pixie frantically waved. "Lower your voice! Do you want the whole neighborhood to hear?"

I had never met one before; I only knew of them from what I'd been told; that they were a secretive culture; that they weren't of this world, exactly; that they were *magic*. I'd heard other things, too. Like, how they were supposed to be divided into the Seelie and the Unseelie; the good and the bad. And how, digging deeper, they were also divided into Courts, with Monarchs, and royalty, and… stuff.

Regular people didn't generally meet the fae; spotting one was a big deal, for common-folk like me.

But that was only the beginning of what the fae really were. They were cruel, and disconnected. They didn't think like humans did. They didn't have our codes of morality or ethics. They worked under a completely different set of rules; rules that made them *dangerous*.

"Are you sure he was fae?" I asked.

"Trust me, they have a distinct smell about them. He was fae."

"Wait… he smelled me, was he trying to figure out what I was?"

"Probably. I don't know."

"But I'm human, though."

"It's totally possible he was actually smelling me, and judging by his face, he probably did."

"Oh shit. No… no, no." I started pacing around my room. "What do you think he'll do? I'm not supposed to have a pixie. *You're* not supposed to be here. Do you think he's told someone? Maybe Madame Whitmore?"

"You need to breathe, right now," Gullie said, hurling soft clouds of fairy dust at me. Though I could feel the beginnings of a second panic attack starting to build, Gullie's magic was doing a good job at fighting the anxiety away.

Slowly, I managed to get my breathing back to normal. I walked over to the window, my hand over my chest, my breaths deep and long. "That was good," I said, "Thank you."

"You're welcome," Gullie said. "I think the important thing for us to do right now is relax, and calm down. Even if he did tell Madame Whitmore what he'd seen, I doubt he could trace you back to her—much less trace you back here. It's gonna be totally fine."

"You're right, it's going to be totally fine."

I took another deep breath at the window, watching the glass fog up with my breathing. Then I noticed something through it. A shimmer of light, like a distortion of air. I narrowed my eyes and wiped the foggy glass with the sleeve of my sweater to look more closely at what was happening in the alley.

My heart almost stopped.

There were people down there. Not just people, but *soldiers* wearing full suits of silver armor, massive silver shields, and gorgeous white capes. Some were wielding swords, others spears, there must've been six or seven of them. No, definitely seven. Three soldiers on either side of one who looked like the leader of the bunch.

He was marching toward the Magic Box… and unsheathing his sword.

"Gullie…" I said, my throat tightening, "I'm going to need more of that powder, now."

Chapter Four

Gullie pressed herself against the window to get a better look at what I was seeing. "Holy crap," she shrieked. "*Fae*. Lots of them."

"*Shit*," I said aloud, heading for my bedroom door. I went to pull it open, I wanted to warn my mothers, but then I remembered. They were gone. Mother Helen had said they'd be immediately leaving for Whitmore Academy. How immediate was *immediately*?

"Are we gonna do something?" Gullie asked.

"I'm thinking!"

"I just can't believe they brought a whole squad down here, and in suits of armor no less! I know pixies aren't supposed to be hanging around humans, but it's not *that* bad a crime."

"I don't think they're here for us, are they? They can't be."

I heard banging on the front door, and a voice calling out. Mother Pepper's super fruit once again proving itself useful. If they weren't yet inside, it meant the front door was locked, and *that* meant my mothers had left the Magic Box. I was alone, here, but I couldn't leave. The soldiers were blocking the only way out of the house.

Maybe if I stayed in my room they'd go away?

"Someone's saying something!" Gullie called out from the window.

I rushed over to her and listened.

"—of the Winter Court of Windhelm, by Royal decree and on behalf of the King, you are hereby ordered to *open this door*." Whoever was speaking emphasized that last part by banging against the door to the Magic Box.

Of course, there was no reply. Nobody was home except me, and like hell I was going to make myself known before I had to.

"We need to get out of here," I whispered.

"Really? Because I was thinking we could hang around, maybe put a kettle on and invite them in for tea."

"Now is *not* the time to be a smartass."

"Then say something clever and I won't have to be!"

I turned to face my bedroom door. They weren't in the house yet. I had time. The only problem was, time for *what*, exactly? I lived in a house of mages; there had to be a closet somewhere full of magic items I could use to fight the fae off, but if such a closet existed, I didn't know about it.

There was only me and my totally human self between them and whatever they'd come here for.

"Do it," I heard someone outside say.

I looked out the window in time to catch one of the fae wind back his arm and hurl a bolt of whooshing energy straight into the side of the house. The walls and the window trembled, dust fell from the ceiling, and then my ears popped. Something had changed; something was *gone*. A moment later, the fae soldier standing by the door kicked it in. I heard the bell jingle, the shattering of glass, the splintering of wood.

They were inside, now.

I ducked behind the window and covered my head with my hands. They were inside. I didn't know who exactly they were, what they wanted, or why they'd come here, but in a moment, they were going to get it, and there was nothing I could do.

"*Please* tell me you have an invisibility cloak in the wardrobe, or something," Gullie begged.

"Oh, yes!" I hissed, "Why didn't I think of that?"

Gullie blinked at me, dumbfounded. "Wait, you have one?"

"Sarcasm!"

I could hear them downstairs, their suits of armor clanking as they rushed through the shop and into the back. One of them was barking to the others not to touch anything, but to spread out and *find her*. Considering there was only one *her* in the building, it had to be me they were talking about. I was starting to think they'd planned to show up at exactly this moment, when my mothers were all out.

"What are we gonna do?" Gullie asked.

"I don't know," I said, "But I'm not gonna let them take us without a fight."

I didn't have anything in the way of weapons, and I didn't own any magic clothes of my own. My mothers would never let me keep any of the spare materials left over after I'd finish a project. So, I was going to have to deal with them all by myself.

Time wasn't on my side. Without many real options, I rushed over to the bedroom door, flung it open, and headed into the adjoining living room. The stairs were narrow, and those guys with their big suits of armor were already going to have a tough time getting through to make it up here.

I needed to block it, somehow, but the heaviest thing I could find was an armchair. With a bit of effort, I dragged it into the stairwell and pushed it toward the edge catching one of the intruders by surprise as he made his way up. When he saw me, he stopped, and jabbed a metal-gloved finger at me.

"You!" he yelled.

I pushed the armchair, making it topple end over end and screaming, "Get out of my house!"

"By order of the Wint—" the armchair bounced on its feet a couple of times before striking the armored soldier, pushing him back down the way he had come and pinning him to the wall at the bottom of the stairwell.

Another soldier came into view at the foot of the stairs, but between the armchair and his downed buddy, who was struggling to get up, he was going to have a hard time getting through. I ran into the kitchen and started grabbing pots, pans, knives; anything I could get my hands on.

Chaos was unfolding at the foot of the stairwell, voices floating wildly around. The armchair was well and truly stuck in its place, and they hadn't succeeded in getting it out of the way by the time I returned to the top of the stairs. With a knife in one hand, and a pot in the other, I struck a defiant pose and glared at the intruders.

"If you don't get out of my house right now," I yelled, "I'm going to rain all kinds of hell on you."

"Don't try to resist!" one soldier called out, "We're here to take you away from this stinking place."

"*Stinking place*? My house smells like a bakery, you cretin!"

I launched a cooking pot at the soldiers, striking one of them on the shoulder. Another pot bounced off his helmet, and even though none of this was going to hurt him any, it was enough to make him retreat around the corner, but I wasn't even given a second to savor my small victory.

The soldier I had squished with the armchair was starting to slide out from under it. I had thought it would hold them for a little longer, but with the help of one of his friends, they had picked it up and were quickly able to shove it out of the way.

With the chair gone, the intruders began their advance.

I held out my knife and backed away as one of the soldiers started marching up the stairs, but the sword in his hand was way bigger and deadlier than the kitchen knife in mine. Still, it was all I had, and I wasn't ready to surrender.

My mothers hadn't raised a wimp.

When he reached the top of the stairs, I found myself entranced by the armor he was wearing. It was a gorgeous, deep blue surrounded by a crisp, white trim with a large set of antlers emblazoned on the breastplate. He wore a long, luxuriant cloak, white on the outside and deep blue on the inside. I couldn't help but admire the stitching, the craftsmanship, it was exquisite.

He raised his sword arm and aimed the tip at my throat. "By the authority of the King of the Winter Court of Arcadia, Yidgam Woflsbane, Lord of Windhelm, Slayer of Giants and Master of the Forge, you are to come with us, or die where you stand."

I couldn't see his face, his helmet covered it all save for his chin and his eyes. But he had a deep, gruff voice, a thick, white beard, sparkling blue eyes, and unusually pale skin. His breath formed in little puffs around his lips as he spoke. I was stunned. I wasn't sure whether to be horrified or blown away with sheer awe.

"*Hello?*" Gullie whispered against my ear, snapping me out of the trance. "Answer him!"

Right.

"I... I don't recognize your authority," I said.

"You don't?"

"The fae have no authority on Earth." That was a rumor I'd heard; one I hoped was true and would get me out of this bind. The fae had their realm, and we had ours; neither had a say in what happened in the other's home.

"I think you'll find my authority to be absolute," he said. "I will give you another chance to come quietly, but I will not ask again."

I swallowed hard. The more the silence between us deepened, the more I noticed my hand was shaking with the weight of the knife I was holding, while his wasn't—despite his sword being larger, and far heavier. His blue eyes, though striking, were also cold, and detached. I was starting to believe this man would *absolutely* kill me if I didn't do as he asked.

Obviously, I didn't want to die, but I wasn't thinking about myself; I was thinking about my mothers, and how devastated they would be if they came home to find me dead.

Frowning, I let the knife fall to the floor. With any luck, my mothers would find the place torn up and come looking for me. I had no way of letting them know where I was going, or even who I was going with, but Mother Helen was the cleverest person I knew. If anyone was going to be able to figure out where I'd been taken, it was her.

"Fine," I said, "You win."

The soldier standing in front of me didn't sheathe his sword. Instead, he stood aside and allowed another of his men to step into the living room and come and fetch me. The room was already small, but the presence of these large, armored men started to make it feel downright cramped, and way too claustrophobic for my liking.

Without speaking, and clearly without any kind of manners or tact, he grabbed my arm and yanked me across the room so hard it almost gave me whiplash. I fell to my knees before the sword of the soldier in charge.

"That's it?" the man who had pulled me said, "*That's* who we have come here to collect?"

"Yes," said the one in charge. He took a deep whiff of the air around me. "This is the one."

"But… look at her. She's so *meek*, and… plain. Even her human glamor is boring, and she truly does stink."

"It's the human world," another said, "Everything stinks. But yes, her, especially."

"Hey!" I protested.

"You will be quiet," said the man in charge, tipping the edge of his sword up to my chin. It was as cold as ice, and as sharp as a razor. "The human world has made you soft, but that will soon change. Speak out of turn, and I will hurt you. If pain does not convince you, I will have you stripped down for the duration of the trip, and you will walk in the cold. Now, stand."

"It's hard to move with this thing stuck to my throat."

Frowning, the soldier pulled it away, and I got to my feet, not once breaking eye contact with my captor. Once I was up, he let the sword fall to his side.

He gestured with his head to the stairs. "Move," he barked. "Try anything, and you will die."

Well, you're just super charming, aren't you?

Taking a deep breath, I started down the steps where more soldiers waited to usher me through the Magic Box and out onto the street. It felt like the temperature around me had dropped a good couple of degrees during the time the fae had spent here. They certainly weren't what I had expected, given the rumors I'd grown up hearing about the fae. Weren't they supposed to be noble, and regal?

These guys were just icy thugs.

"This way, whelp," said a soldier standing just outside the busted door to the Magic Box.

I was being carried away by armed men, and all I could do was worry about someone breaking into the shop now that the door was broken. "What about—"

"—*this way*," he repeated, pointing at a shimmering point of light somewhere around the middle of the alley.

I started walking, escorted by three soldiers, with the others not far behind. The closer I got to the shimmering cloud, the colder the air seemed to get. By the time I reached it, I was shivering, my lips chattering, my limbs quaking. The cobblestones around the strange ripple in the air looked frozen solid.

"What is this?" I asked.

"Walk through," a soldier barked.

"Through… *that*?"

"This attitude is starting to get boring." came another voice, this one smooth, and deep… and almost disinterested. I knew who had spoken before I even looked. It was *him*. The guy from earlier. The guy who had grabbed me and… sniffed me. It was the weirdest, sexiest, most random thing that had ever happened to me, but today was full of random, wasn't it?

I turned my head to the side just enough to see him. Unlike the others, he wasn't wearing armor—he looked very much like a human. A human who owned private jets and expensive cars, but still human. Still… gorgeous.

Shit.

Why did my kidnapper also have to be gorgeous?

"It's you," I said, the words falling out of my mouth on a shivering sigh.

He stared at me, his icy eyes cold and uncaring. "Do as you're told, and you will be unharmed," he said.

"Unharmed? You're kidnapping me, and you destroyed my shop. The harm has been done, you… you *cockwomble*."

He turned to the man standing next to him. Without having to say a word, the soldier gave him his sword, which he then aimed at the ground beneath my feet. He looked at me, his eyes low and narrow.

"I don't care enough to threaten you," he said, "So, instead, I'll ask you. Once. Go through the portal, now."

I stared at him, grinding my teeth, but tears promised to spill from my eyes if I kept looking at him. I turned away from him and went back to looking at the portal in the alley. Shutting my eyes, and without another word, I took a step forward—and the world fell out from under me.

Chapter Five

A brutal, bitter wind bit deep into my face the moment I came out on the other side of the portal. My stomach had twisted into itself, my entire body felt like it had been dipped into an icy lake. Even before I opened my eyes, I knew, I wasn't in London anymore. The air was too cold, but more importantly, it was too fresh—too wild.

Then I opened my eyes, and my mouth fell open.

A vast landscape of snowy cliffs and huge, white mountains rolled away from me in all directions. Air currents dragged fingers of condensation into the sky at their peaks. The wind howled as it pushed past me, rushing through my hair and over my shoulders, carrying with it a flurry of snow... and maybe even faint, distant whispers.

I'd never seen anything like this before, had never been anywhere like this; somewhere so primal and natural, but also so... empty. There was nothing out here, only rolling, icy hills and jagged mountains as far as the eye could see.

Something snorted nearby, and I jumped at the sound, my bones nearly leaping out of my skin. It was a huge white elk-type-thing with enormous, white antlers and a full, thick coat that was so silky it seemed to glitter in the sunlight.

I stared at the beast, my eyes wide, my heart thumping against my chest. Then another one moved into view, trotting lightly over the snow. When it shook its head, its entire body moved. I was so fixed on the creatures and how beautiful they were that I hadn't noticed the reins attached to their bodies, and the massive silvery carriage they were attached to.

Seated atop the carriage was a man wearing a furry grey coat. He had long, black hair, bright eyes the color of the wintery sky above us, and… pointed ears… and a pair of thin, curved antlers that followed the shape of his head. He stared at me from where he sat from behind disinterested eyes.

A hand wrapped around my shoulder and someone shoved me toward the carriage. "Move," said a gruff, deep voice.

I was already shivering, the cold easily working its way into my bones. Sitting in the carriage probably wasn't a bad idea, so I walked over to it. On the outside, the ornate carriage looked like it, too, was made of ice. The entire body glittered as I approached. But inside, it was blessedly warm, and comfortable.

I sat down on the black, velvety seats, and started rubbing my hands together, blowing into them for warmth. Three soldiers joined me, their full suits of armor clanking as they settled into their seats. The last one in shut the door, and then the soldier across from me knocked the wall with his fist a couple of times.

A moment later, the carriage started moving. Interestingly, the guy in the suit hadn't joined us in this carriage. If I had to hazard a guess as to why that was, I'd say it was probably because he was too important to ride around in a carriage with the likes of me. I couldn't say I was upset about that. There was no telling what would happen to me if I had to look at him again right now.

The man sitting across from me didn't let his gaze slip once. He was fixed on me, watching my every move, studying me. "Why do you do that with your hands?" he asked.

"For warmth," I said.

"Why do you need to be warm?"

I cocked an eyebrow. "You're kidding, right?"

"She's spent too long in the human world," another one of the soldiers said, "Her blood is weak."

"Too long in the… *what*?"

"Let us be glad we are out of that place," the third soldier said. "I cannot stand Earth… and *humans*. Why must they smell so? If it were up to me, they would all be slaves."

"Hey, wait a second," I snapped, "Why do you have to slag humans off? What did we ever do to you?"

"*We*," the one across from me, the leader of the group, said, "Look at her. She thinks she's one of them."

"That's because I—" a sharp, stabbing pain at the base of my neck shut me down so hard I almost bit my own tongue. Wincing, I shut up. That had been Gullie's work. I'd forgotten she was even there. My instinct was to snap at her, too, but I knew better than to keep talking after that.

I decided to take the soldier, and I guess Gullie's, advice and remain quiet for the rest of the trip to… wherever we were going. They'd called it Windhelm, in *Arcadia*. I didn't know much about it, only rumors and whatever stories my mothers had told me.

Arcadia, I knew, was the name of the realm to which all the fae belonged. It was their world; a vast and wonderous place, with continents, and oceans, countries, and nations. Nobody else lived in Arcadia, only the fae. It wasn't that the fae realm was inhospitable to humans, it was that the fae themselves hated the idea of sharing their land with those *not of the blood* and took steps to make sure humans found in Arcadia were… removed.

Another thing I'd heard the soldiers mention was the Winter Court. As far as I knew, the Courts were like fae factions. They were the cultures of the fae world, the nations. The Winter Court, the Summer Court; Spring, Autumn. Each had its own land, its own rules, customs, and leaders.

If that was true, if these other factions existed, I couldn't help but wonder why in the hell it had to have been the Winter Court that had snatched me up and not, say, the Summer Court? I'd never left England. I'd never even left London. I was used to the cold, but if I was going to be kidnapped by fae, why couldn't I have been taken somewhere a little warmer?

Shit.

That was the first time I had even thought the word.

I had been kidnapped; kidnapped by fae who rode giant elk and carried swords that were as cold as ice. This was all starting to feel like a fever dream, and maybe it was. Maybe I'd fallen asleep in my workroom, and if I shook myself hard enough, I'd wake up. I decided not to try it, just in case one of the soldiers around me thought I was being threatening.

Me.

Threatening.

I wasn't sure how long we spent in the carriage. After a while, the landscape rolling by, as beautiful as it was, started to just look… white. Yes, the cliffs and the mountains were a sight to behold, but there really wasn't much more to it than that. Luckily, all of this vast nothingness and silence gave me time to think.

I needed to figure a way out of this mess, but with three soldiers around me and the only exit blocked, there were none. I also hadn't considered exactly what I'd do if I did somehow manage to jump out of the carriage and make a run for it.

Where would I run to? Where would I find shelter? How long until the cold dragged me into death?

I needed to keep my wits about me, look for opportunities, and carefully consider my actions and my words. My mothers would've returned home by now. They would know I had been taken, and they would start looking for me. My only objective was to stay alive and wait for them to find me.

I took a deep breath of that crisp, cold air and looked out of the window again, watching the world roll by. Then the carriage turned a corner, and for the second time today, my jaw dropped. It was like a jewel gleaming in the snow—no, not just one jewel, a whole heap of them dazzling under the sunlight.

It looked like a city, with huge domes and tall spires; all white, all glittering. A single, narrow bridge looked like the only way into and out of the city, which stood like an island against the surrounding cliffs and mountains. It was the most beautiful place I had ever seen, majestic, regal, and proud—but also cold, and… *lonely*. There was nothing around this marvelous city, only more jagged peaks, and snow.

There was something sad about that.

"Is this… Windhelm?" I asked.

The man sitting across from me didn't answer. He only stared at me some more, his bright eyes fixed.

I nodded. "I guess I'll take that as a yes," I said.

The carriage drew ever closer to the city as the minutes ticked away. Soon enough, we were on the bridge, which made for a much smoother ride compared to the ground we'd been on. Even from inside the carriage I got a sense of just how high up the bridge was from the deepest point beneath it. The entire city looked like it was on a natural plateau, elevated from the rest of the world, kept apart from it.

We didn't halt at the gates; the carriage instead being waved through by another soldier-type fae on the ground. Clearly, we were expected. As the carriage rolled through the stony streets, flanked on both sides by white buildings that glittered like they were made of ice, the soldier across from me decided to speak.

"These are the rules," he said. "You do not speak unless spoken to. You dress the way we tell you to. You eat what we give you. And you don't try to escape. If you attempt to escape, we will not hunt you down. We will not send soldiers looking for you. The nearest town is several hundreds of miles away. You will not survive without help, and you will find none of that in Windhelm. Do you understand?"

"I understand I've just been kidnapped," I said, "You realize people will come looking for me, right? Powerful people."

"They will never find you here. And if they did, they would freeze to death trying to break through our defenses."

"I'm pretty sure you shouldn't underestimate mages."

The soldier to my right scoffed. "Mages are little more than children who've learned to pick their nose, compared to us," he said.

The leader of the group flicked his wrist, and a white flame rolled along the palm of his hand. It danced and weaved through his fingers in a dazzling display. "Mages play with magic they cannot hope to comprehend during their small, short lives," he said, "We *are* magic. We are fae."

I was getting a little sick of their uppity attitudes, but I had to contain my dislike. Playing along was the only way I was going to get through this, and short of being asked to do something horrible, I was going to play along as much as I could. I didn't have another choice.

Finally, the carriage stopped.

"Where are we?" I asked.

"You have already broken the first rule," the soldier said, a low rumble in his throat. "Be quiet and get out."

Already the other soldiers were filing out of the carriage, clearing the way for me to step off and finally set foot in this cold, wonderful, *dangerous* city.

The cobbles shone like they were slick and slippery. I was careful stepping onto them, hoping I wouldn't fall flat on my arse as soon as my feet touched the ground. I didn't. The ground was firm beneath my feet, and beside a little nip in the air, I wasn't feeling the cold as bad as I had been when I first arrived in Arcadia.

The wind whispered through my hair as I looked around, gawking at just how tall those domes and spires were. I'd never seen buildings as tall as the ones surrounding me. It was enough to make me feel small, truly small, and maybe that was the point?

The soldier in charge jabbed me in the back with his metal elbow and nearly sent me skidding across the street. I glared at him, but I also bit my tongue and kept my mouth shut. Turning around to walk again, I realized he'd shoved me toward a massive white door set into a wall of pure-white ice.

The door stood at the top of a set of grand, wide stairs flanked on both sides by icy columns in the shape of lanterns. I wasn't sure exactly where we were, after a while all the buildings started looking the same, but this one had a certain grandiose quality about it, like a church, or a… a castle.

I walked up the stairs, careful not to move too quickly along them, just in case. Behind me marched all seven of the soldiers that had invaded the Magic Box, their capes billowing with the wind. The door ahead of me bore the same antler regalia the soldiers all wore on their armor. It opened as I reached it, even if there wasn't anyone there to push it, but it didn't open all the way.

The closer I got, the more I wanted to stop moving. It was like pressure building against my chest, my temples, my arms. There was magic at work, here. I'd grown up around it, I knew how it felt, what it could look like, how it could sound—and more importantly, how it could make you feel. This was a barrier, I'd reached; something meant to keep people out.

People like me.

"Be on your best behavior," the lead soldier snarled, and then opened the doors and shoved me through them. This time, I couldn't keep my footing. I scrambled, flailed, and ultimately fell on my face on a cold, sleek floor of deep blue marble, or stone.

The fall had winded me, and it took a minute for me to find my strength and get back up again. Ultimately, it was the cold of the floor that encouraged me to stand upright. I felt like a deer taking her first few steps, totally unbalanced, my *Earth* shoes struggling to find any sort of grip on the smooth ground.

The door had shut behind me, and the soldiers hadn't followed. I was rid of them, wherever I was, so I flipped them off, shoving both my middle fingers toward the door and hurling all manner of obscenities that bounced off the walls around me like gunshots.

Then someone coughed, and I froze, sucking in a sharp breath through my teeth. Slowly, I turned. Someone was there. Someone had seen what I'd done, and I was probably going to be in some trouble for it. There was one thing I knew you shouldn't do to the fae, and that was offend or insult them.

My mouth dropped again. There were *hundreds* of people, all gathered along grand balconies and stalls stretching for what felt like miles, and they were all staring at me. I was standing in front of the entire

Winter Court, and I'd just flipped off and cursed out a bunch of their soldiers.

A lot.

"Ah... *shit.*"

Chapter Six

The mind does weird things when you're put under immense pressure. Me? I remembered my first ever school play. I was seven years old. The play itself had been a production of Jack and the Beanstalk, and I had the privilege of playing the *beanstalk*. I had a minor speaking role, but through most of the play, I just had to stand there and not move, not talk—not until the very end, when Jack cut me down with his axe.

Argh! You've chopped me down!

That was all I had to say, and I managed to screw that up by seizing up just as I was supposed to start speaking. Jack had pretended to hit me with his axe, my cue was up, and all I could do was stand there and stare blankly into the audience. *Panic*. Utter terror of messing it up prevented me from saying a word. It took an actual strike of the plastic axe against my shin for me to finally say something. Anything.

That was the first time I'd ever yelled *shit*, and it had the entire crowd in stitches.

Thinking about it, the kid who played Jack was a bit of a dick. He hadn't really had to hit me, but he'd done it anyway, and then he'd laughed about it.

Already too many seconds had passed since I'd made my grand entrance into this grandiose, domed hall, and I still hadn't said another word. Sunlight filtered in from high above and caught on just about every glittery silver dress; every sharp, frost-white right angle; every piece of jewelry that was out on display.

It looked like the entire court was here, a sea of blank, ice-cold faces staring at me from all over. They were all immaculately dressed and *so* ridiculously attractive. Each face was as beautiful and as striking than the one next to it, if not more so. But they were only observers to what was going on at the center of the great hall.

A whole host of women stood side by side, each wearing fine, silver dresses of shifting mercury. Some of them had curved antlers growing out of their temples, others iridescent wings, but each one of them looked like snow princesses; snow princesses standing in front of the Royal Court… and the King.

No one, not a soul in here, was in *stitches*.

"*Girl*," came a booming voice that filled the domed hall and echoed along its walls, "Move closer."

For a moment, I couldn't. I was frozen, like my younger self had been. Seven-year-old me wasn't under imminent threat of death, though, so I swallowed hard and, taking it one step at a time, started walking along the smooth floor beneath my feet.

Sometimes it was more of a slide than a walk, but I made it work as best I could and didn't fall over. That was important. I'd already made a fool of myself once, I wasn't about to do it again. At least, that was the plan.

Each of the Winter Courtiers sparkled like they were ice sculptures. None of them moved much, except to start whispering as I walked past them and toward the line of *fifteen* women standing before the Royals. I couldn't hear what they were saying, but they were talking about me. A couple had even started giggling, which just did wonders for my already crippling stage fright.

I stopped when I reached the other women and glanced across at the one next to me. Beautiful didn't even begin to describe her. In fact, that word probably did her a disserve because of how common a word it was. Her skin was pale and flawless, her cheeks shimmered as the light touched them, and her hair looked like it was made of pure, white silk. That was to say nothing about those ice blue eyes, her button nose, or her adorably proportionate antlers.

I'd never in my life seen people like this; they made even Madame Whitmore look like a busted, old cabbage that had been run over by a car.

"Uh, hi…" I said, already breaking the *don't speak unless spoken to* rule.

The fae next to me scowled, rolled her eyes, and turned her attention to the Royal Court directly ahead of us.

"Now that we are *all* gathered," came that same, booming voice; a voice that didn't seem to come from anyone on the Royal balcony but from all around. "We may commence."

Commence? Commence what?

"Welcome, Courtiers," called the voice, "To the King's Court of Windhelm."

Glittering, shimmering applause erupted all around. As the fae clapped, their outfits, makeup, and wings all drank the sunlight falling from the giant skylight above and sent it streaking in all directions. It was mesmerizing to watch, like being in a cave filled with millions of diamonds all fighting to be the brightest.

"Today," said the voice, "Is a joyous day, a proud day… for today marks the beginning of the Royal Selection. This is a time for competition, a time for entertainment, and a time for champions to be born. Each of the young women assembled before us are about to embark on the most important trials of their lives; the ultimate test of character, of strength, of will. They have spent years training for this moment, years preparing for what will be their definitive—or final—moments. These young women will show us what it means to be exceptional, what it means to be determined, but most importantly, they will show us what it means to be members of the Winter Court."

More applause thundered throughout the great hall, but I could barely hear it over the sound of my own pounding heart. Whoever was speaking had said a bunch of words I didn't like. *Competition. Trials. Final moments.* My head was spinning, my hands trembling, my knees buckling. I felt like a snowflake melting on a rock, like I could sink into the floor at any second and become a puddle of water.

Come to think of it, that was probably better than standing here, watching my life flash before my eyes.

"In the days to come," the voice continued, "You will all have the chance to marvel at these incredible women as they undertake their trials. Those who have prepared for everything will thrive, and possibly succeed. Those who have not, may perish. In the end, there can only be one true winner, and her prize shall be two-fold."

Prize?

"The winner shall ascend to the rank of Royal. As a warrior of great skill, she will lead our armies into battle against our foes and bring the deep freeze of Winter to those who oppose and have opposed us. But she will not do it alone, for hers shall also be the honor—the privilege—of having the Prince's hand in marriage."

Another round of clapping ensued, only this time there was a little more to it. I noticed movement on the Royal balcony, a slight shuffling of feet. Several people were standing up, the clapping rising with them.

The first person I noticed was the woman dressed in a sheer white, shimmering gown. Her hair was soft teal, a set of thin, pointed white antlers curled around her head, breaking away from her crown at the sides like

Elk's horns. She wore herself like a Queen, her chin raised high, her eyes wide and all-seeing, her posture exquisite.

Beside her was a bear of a man easily a head taller than the Queen. Broad shouldered, and covered in a thick, furry, black cloak, he surveyed the court from behind intense, sky-blue eyes that seemed to pierce the very soul of the people they touched. He examined the women standing in a line to my right, paying each of them a moment of his attention… and visibly *sneering* with disgust when he saw me; as if I'd offended him, somehow, just by existing.

Then I saw the man who had come up beside them, and my world flipped upside down once more. It was *him*, the guy I'd bumped into, the one who'd sniffed my hair, the fae I'd called a cockwomble. He looked a little differently than he had on Earth—his hair was just as long and curly, and still as dark as the deepest night, but like his mother, he also had thin, white horns that followed the curve of his head.

Shit.

Holy shit.

What the hell was he doing here? What the hell had he been doing in London moments before I'd been captured? Why the hell did he have to be the Prince of the Winter Court? And why was I destined to make an idiot of myself in front of Royalty?

Sure, they were also kidnappers, but mostly, they were Royalty.

"My fellow Courtiers," the voice started up again, "I give you King Yidgam, Queen Haera, and Prince Cillian Wolfsbane, our Lords and protectors, and rulers of Windhelm."

Mention of their names required applause fit for a King and his family. I almost couldn't bare it. I hadn't said a word, and already I knew I was neck deep in pig shit. What prowess did I have? I wasn't a warrior, I certainly wasn't exceptional, and I could with all honesty say I hadn't spent a single minute of my life preparing for these *trials*.

My mothers would've told me if they'd known I was going to be one day kidnapped by fae, sent to Arcadia, and made to compete against other, clearly superior women. But they hadn't, and with good reason, too; I was human, not one of the fae.

They had the wrong girl.

Someone, somewhere, had made a *royal* mistake.

It took everything I had to open my mouth to speak, but I made my lips part and forced my throat to work— only before I could get a word out, Gullie pulled hard on some of my hairs, catching my attention.

"Don't you dare speak," she said, "Not to me, not to them." Her voice was so low, I could barely hear her over the roaring applause. Luckily, she was inches away from my ear, and determined to make sure I heard what she had to say.

I nodded, but only slightly—enough to let her know I'd heard her.

"This is bad," Gullie said, "Really bad. I know I don't have to tell you, but I really needed to get that off my chest. Now, you've got to listen very closely, because I'm not gonna get another chance to speak. These people will *kill* you if you tell them you're human, understand?"

Again, I nodded. A slight movement that, I hoped, hadn't caught anyone's eye—least of all the Prince's.

"They won't send you back," Gullie said, "You've already seen too much of the world, and they're too secretive to take the chance that you won't blab about what you've seen. They're also too lazy to wipe your memory. Killing people is basically their first answer to most problems—all these Unseelie are alike. Whatever happens, you need to go along with this, at least until we can figure out how to get out of here. Nod again if you agree."

A third nod, one that, this time, the girl next to me spotted. She gave me a sidelong glance, her eyes narrow and quizzical. I smiled at her, and she shook her head disgust, then looked away. When I looked over at the Royal Balcony again, the King and Queen were both watching the other women... but the Prince?

His eyes were fixed on me.

I looked at my feet, taking my gaze away from him, but I couldn't keep them there. I had to look back up at him. He'd moved to the edge of the balcony, and he was staring at me, which made sense; the girls next to me were all decked up in fae finery, while I looked like I'd just leapt out of a fabric bin at a pound-shop.

I couldn't tell whether he was intrigued, revolted, or amused by all of this, but it was probably all of the above.

"Now," the speaking voice caught my attention again, "Competitors will retire to their quarters where they will eat and prepare for the first round of trials, beginning tomorrow at dawn. On behalf of the Royal family and the entire court, *may the fates shine on you*."

A final round of clapping erupted. The contestants—*combatants*—were quickly ushered away by a group of soldiers who escorted us all through a door and into a sparkling white hallway. After a short walk, we were led to a luxuriant, white, spacious waiting room filled with couches to lounge on, tables covered in food and drink, and an incredible view of the snowy landscape beyond Windhelm's walls.

I took one look at the corridor behind me, and for an instant wondered if I'd reach the outside if I made a mad dash for the exit.

No, they'd probably kill me.

That kind of death was probably going to be quicker and less painful than dying in some fae trial, but I wasn't ready to die just yet. I needed to stick it out, to survive until my mothers could find me. That was the only way I was going to get out of here.

Sighing, defeated, I stepped through the door, and joined the other girls.

TAKEN (THE COLDEST FAE, BOOK 1)

Chapter Seven

It was a weird thing to feel like you were being totally overlooked, while simultaneously the center of attention. The two seemed impossible, especially considering the way some of the people in here looked.

Everyone was gorgeous, stunning, and decked out in incredible finery the likes of which I probably would never have seen in my lifetime. Meanwhile I looked like I'd fallen out of the back of a lorry filled with awkwardness and mediocrity.

Despite everyone having at least one eye on me, the girls I'd walked into the room with quickly formed little groups and went around claiming places to sit. No one touched the food, although that was probably going to surprise few. The last thing you'd expect to find a group of supermodels doing was attacking a buffet.

I, on the other hand, was starving. I hadn't eaten since this morning, and *since* this morning I had been humiliated, splashed on, kidnapped, and dragged into some strange competition in a frozen fairy land. I clearly had a lot to process, and I hadn't been given enough time to process it.

I wanted to eat, but I also wanted to leave so I could avoid having any contact with these girls.

I decided I would be safest near the buffet area. They were already watching me, judging me. Whether I had food in my mouth or not wasn't going to make a difference. So, I moved across the room toward it, fully aware of the many, many judgmental eyes plastered to my back.

I tried to tune it out. This wasn't, after all, my first rodeo. I'd grown up being the weird one in school, the pasty girl with no friends and weird hobbies, the one who wore turn of the century clothes instead of modern ones because they made her feel more comfortable, more like herself.

The girl with the three mothers.

That last one was a point of much ridicule during my younger days. My mothers had never tried to dress the situation to look like anything that it wasn't. I knew my real parents were gone, and that Mother Helen, Mother Pepper, and Mother Evie had taken up the responsibility of being my guardians from a very young age. They were proud to have all become my mothers, and never tried to hide that pride.

They, however, weren't the ones getting it in school. I tried to keep it from them; the name-calling, the bullying. If Mother Helen had the power to turn me into a frog for a while to teach me a lesson, there was no telling what she'd do to a child she thought was making her daughter sad. She was always a staunch defender of mine; the fierce old lioness who didn't take anyone else's shit—least of all from her own offspring, whether adopted or not.

I missed them. I needed them. I was on my own out here, relying purely on my own instincts and thick skin to get me through. And I was going to need all the instinct and thick skin I could manage, because three of the girls in the room were heading right for me.

I'd already picked up a crescent shaped object that looked like a small puff pastry covered in powdered sugar before I realized I was being set upon by beautiful hyenas. I quickly placed it back on its plate and wiped my fingertips against my clothes before turning to face them head on.

Calm yourself, Dahlia, I thought, *they're more scared of you than you are of them.*

Shit, that's bears, not fae.

Double shit.

"Hello, little one," one of the approaching three girls said. She pouted. "You look… lost. May we help you find your way out?"

It was always the prettiest ones that cut the deepest, and this girl was the most breathtaking female I'd ever laid eyes on, besides the Queen. Her skin was so fair, it was almost unreal. She had sky-blue hair held in a perfect updo, with wild, rogue strands falling around her face to perfectly frame it. And her horns, instead of white like many of the other girls, were black, and thick, and they curled around her head like a crown.

With her dress of shifting mercury and all her rings, and earrings, and finery, I could tell this one was going to be trouble.

"I'm fine where I am," I said, keeping my defenses up. I eyed the other two girls up and down. One of them sneered.

"She smells like the human world," one said.

"She looks human, too," the other one put in. "Why does she look human?"

"Now, now," queen bee said, "There's no need to throw barbs at the poor thing. Tell me, what is your name?"

"Dahlia," I said, "What's yours?"

"Mareen," she said, offering a slight bow of her head, "My father is the Master of Rites here."

Pretend like you know what that means. "Oh, sure. That's great."

"These are my friends Kali, and Verrona." Her eyebrows fluttered. "So, what does your father do?"

My eyes darted around the room, settling finally on the table covered with food—specifically on the pastry that had reminded me of Mother Pepper. "He's a baker. My mother is a seamstress."

"That is so, absolutely *cute*," Mareen beamed. "Did your father prepare any of the food here today?"

She was trying to figure out if I was important, if I was just some random who'd wandered in here off the street, or worse, if I was the *joke* contestant. I couldn't tell her the truth about who I was, I also didn't know enough about this place to lay down a convincing lie, so instead I decided to make up an outrageous lie.

"He didn't, because he's… not here. He's undercover. In… the human world."

"Undercover?" she cocked her head to the side, "Whatever do you mean?"

I could've cringed at what I was about to say, but I couldn't think of any other line to defend myself with. "I could tell you… but then I'd have to kill you."

I'd just quoted a line from a movie. I could only hope they didn't have access to Satellite TV out here.

Mareen, Kali, and Verrona all stared at me, wide eyed, their thin necks craning backwards slightly, none of them looking like they were even breathing. They each glanced at each other, scanning one another's eyes, and then promptly burst into a fit of laughter that exploded into the room.

It turned out their laughter was infectious. Soon, other fae were laughing, even if they couldn't possibly have heard what we were saying unless they had incredible hearing. Then again, everyone in here had pointed ears, so, anything was possible, I guess.

Blood and anger flushed into my cheeks. I scowled at them. "You don't believe me?" I asked, daring to raise my voice above the laughter.

It took a moment for Mareen to come back down, but when she did, she allowed her poise to return. "That was the funniest thing I've heard in a very long time," she said. "I must thank you."

"Don't thank me," I said. "I was being serious. You have no idea who I am, where I'm from, or who my parents are. You only know what I look like, and I look human, which means my story could hold water. Maybe I have the power to kill you, maybe I'm bluffing. I was brought here for a reason, though."

"True. You *are* here, and that's not insignificant or by mistake. But I doubt it's because you have the power to kill anyone." Her soft, thin lips curled into a smile. "I think you're here because even a performance as serious as the Royal Selection needs a joke or two to lighten the tone from time to time. Make no mistake, you won't get past the opening trial, but you'll definitely be remembered fondly for giving everyone a good chuckle or two… and for smelling and looking like a rat drowned in vomit."

I frowned at her. I was about to launch into a furious, wordy attack, but I held myself. That's exactly what she wanted. She wanted me to yell at her, to insult her, to throw my verbal anger at her walls so she could show everyone else just how little it hurt.

This was all about dominance for her. Mareen wanted to find the person she could most easily push around and make a big show of it. She was already playing the game, but she was playing it wrong.

If she really wanted to make a show of strength, she should've gone to the nastiest looking girl in the room, maybe the one with the turquoise hair, hurling whole apple-sized fruits into her mouth and chomping them down like they were grapes. She wasn't just beautiful; she was also fit, and strong—feminine, yet muscular.

She could've snapped Mareen in half, and that was why I had been her target.

"You know what?" I asked.

"What?" she said, smiling sweetly.

"You're not as pretty as you think. You're not as graceful as you think. And I'm wearing a human glamor right now. I can, and will, look better than I do, where you can only look worse. Good luck handling that when the time comes."

She frowned, the very few, and soft lines of her face deepening. It looked like she was about to say something, when the door to the room opened and a woman called for Kali. The three turned around to look at the door, and at the woman standing there. "It's time," the woman said, extending her hand.

Kali looked at Mareen and at Verrona, nodded, wished them luck, and then left. One by one, all the other girls in the room were called by a different fae who came to pluck them out of the room. Were they being taken to their first trials? I had no way of knowing. All I could do was wait until my own number came up; or didn't.

Maybe this really had been all one big mistake, and I would be left here on my own until someone found me and went, *hey, you're not supposed to be here.*

Thinking about it, that probably wouldn't turn out well for me. I was a human in the world of the fae. I doubted if anyone would give me a second look before deciding my life was forfeit just for being here. Least of all the Prince. I got the feeling he was more of the murdering type than the listening type.

The contestants were called out of the room pretty much in quick succession, one after the other. There weren't even a couple of moments of pause between one girl leaving, and another being asked to leave. I was the last one in the room, and for a moment I thought no one would come, but a woman finally did.

She, like the just about everyone else in this damn place, was beautiful, and pale. Hair as white as snow, eyes a vibrant violet, and skin that looked like it had never encountered even a single blemish. This fae also had antlers running along her head, although hers were short—barely more than finger-length.

The woman at the door recoiled a little, a sneer on her face. I was getting used to that by now, but it would never *not* suck. "You're Dahlia?" she asked.

I looked around at the empty room. "I was the last time I checked," I said.

"Right…" she said, pausing. "Well, come this way."

I didn't argue with her. All the other girls had been taken away, and that meant wherever I was going, it probably wasn't the chopping block. Then again, this was the land of the fae; nothing was certain, and there was always more than met the eye.

KATERINA MARTINEZ

Chapter Eight

The suite I was brought to put my bedroom *and* workroom to shame. The space was wide, and open, and bright, with a couch to lounge on, a bed five times the size of my own bed at home, and a wardrobe fit for a Queen. Across from the door, a huge bay window looked out upon a glittering courtyard filled with *trees*; giant, snow-covered trees.

The fae who had led me here walked past me and into the center of the room, where she gestured around herself.

"Welcome to your room," she said.

"My... my room?" I asked.

"Of course, this is where you will be staying for the duration of the Royal Selection. My name is Mira, I am your Custodian."

"Custodian? Like, my keeper?"

She shook her head, her soft white curls delicately waving while she moved. "Not quite a keeper. I am bound to your service so long as you are a participant in the Royal Selection. My duties are to tend to your needs, answer any questions you may have, and ensure you have the best possible chance of being victorious in your quest for the Prince's hand, and glory untold."

I cocked an eyebrow. It sounded like a well-rehearsed speech, more than something said from the heart. She had a kind of distant look about her, like she was only barely present, and only slightly interested in what was going on. Then again, so did every other bloody person around here.

I frowned at her. "So, you're saying your job is to make sure I win?"

"That's right. I am to heal your wounds, see to your attire, and provide you with advice, should you request it. I am forbidden from doing anything that may jeopardize your chances of succeeding. In fact, your success would bring me and my family great honor."

"Forbidden…" I prodded, "Forbidden, how?"

She looked at me with quizzical eyes, as if she couldn't understand why I was asking such a simple question. "Custodians are bound by magic to serve," she said, then paused, "You aren't quite like the others, are you?"

"What gave it away?"

She gave me an *up and down* kind of look, then pointed at my skirt. "Those don't look like regular clothes."

"They are where I come from."

"The human world?"

I took a desperate few steps toward Mira, only to have her flinch like I was covered in horse crap. "I have something I need to tell someone. Anyone. And I think you're the person."

"I don't understand."

"If I tell you something that could hurt my chances of winning these trials, would magic stop you from repeating it to anyone else?"

She stared at me, blankly, "Well... yes. Fate itself forbids me. But, why would you tell me something that could hurt your chances of winning?"

I took a deep breath, then paused, waiting for a pull of hair or a sharp stabbing sensation. It didn't come, and that meant Gullie—at least on the surface—approved of what I was about to do. On the back of a single breath, I spat it all out.

"My name is Dahlia Crowe, and a couple of hours ago I was taken from my home at sword-point and brought here, made to ride in a carriage being pulled by giant elk, and then thrown in front of the King and all the Royals or whatever, and now I'm expected to take part in a trial that I haven't prepared for."

I exhaled, then continued.

"I don't know any magic, I've never even hit a person, and I certainly don't have the experience to lead an army. I don't know who's in charge of finding the people who are supposed to take part in this Royal Selection, but someone has made a huge mistake picking me up, and they should definitely lose their job for it."

Mira's eyes were wide, violet ovals. This time it was *her* jaw that dropped, a little. "What… what are you saying?"

"I don't belong here, okay? I'm a human."

"*Human*!?"

I wrapped one hand around her mouth and the other around the back of her head. "Could you *possibly* say that any louder? I don't quite think the King heard you!"

Mira muffled into my hand. I'd expected her breath to be cold against my palm, but it was warm, just like mine.

"I'm gonna need you to listen for a second," I said, "Only nod or shake your head, understood?"

Mira nodded, her eyes wide and deer-like.

"I don't know how this happened," I continued, "I was at home, bothering no one, when a bunch of your people barged in with swords and took me. They didn't ask to know who I was, they didn't wait to get permission from my parents before taking me — it was a straight kidnapping. I don't know who you all think I am, but I'm not her, and I need to go home. Will you help me?"

She stared at me, not moving at first, then she frowned.

"What does that mean?" I asked. She didn't reply, then I realized she couldn't speak even if she wanted to.

"I'm about to remove my hand. Do you promise not to scream or tell anyone about what I've just told you?"

A nod. I released her mouth. She didn't say anything, instead she watched me, her head slowly arching to the side, her eyes narrowing. "I... I don't understand."

"What don't you understand? Whoever I'm supposed to be, I'm not her."

"But you're... you're fae."

"I can assure you, I'm not."

"You smell fae."

I turned my head slightly. "Gullie, you can come out, I think."

Gullie's wings buzzed, and the little pixie shot out of my hair, making the fae stiffen up again. "*Harpy*," she hissed.

"Excuse me," Gullie said, "But I'm a *pixie*, not a harpy. There's a big difference."

Mira pointed at Gullie. "You're not supposed to be here. Your kind are forbidden from entering our city."

"So are humans, and yet," Gullie cocked her thumb at me.

"She is not human. You *are* a harpy."

"*Pixie*."

I shook my head. "You're not getting the message, Mira. I am human. The only reason why you think I'm fae is because she's been living in my hair."

Mira turned to look at me, confusion written all over her face. She inched her nose a little closer to me and, once the pixie dust had cleared, took a whiff of the air around me. I thought that would've made things clearer for her, but she only looked more confused after that.

Confused, and a little disgusted.

"You… you are human," she said, trailing off.

"See? That's what I've been trying to tell you."

"But… you are also fae. I can smell it."

"What you're smelling is me," Gullie said, "My scent, her scent, it's all mixed up. Trust me, if I stayed away from her long enough, you'd probably only smell human on her."

"Fantastic," Mira exclaimed, throwing her arms up. "Just *fantastic*."

"What is?" I asked.

"This! *All of this*. Do you have any idea how long I've been preparing to be a Custodian? My family aren't Royals, you know. We're just regular old folks, trying to make an honest living." Mira started pacing around the room, talking to herself but looking at me. It was as if she'd snapped, and I'd watched it happen right in front of me. "My father does his best, you know? He's a carpenter… that means he makes furniture."

"I know what a carpenter is," I scowled.

She jabbed a finger at me and growled. "Hush, *drummenir*."

"Droo—what?"

Mira hadn't heard me. Instead, she kept rambling. "You see, my father… he's getting long in the tooth, so I decided to train to be a Custodian. There's honor in that, there's *wealth* in that. If I do a good enough job, my family can live comfortably for the rest of their days. All I have to do is ensure you make it as long as possible in these trials. The longer you make it, the better it is for me."

"Seems like a pretty easy job."

"Three years I've trained for this," she continued, ignoring me. "Three whole years I could've been helping with our family business. Instead, I spent that time educating myself in the rigorous rituals of the Winter Court, meticulously improving my poise, my stature, my overall aesthetic appeal, all getting ready for this moment… and I get the *broken* one."

I scowled. "Hey, who are you calling the broken one?"

She pointed at me. "*You* are! Not only do you clearly have no training whatsoever that could help you in these trials, but you're also *drummenir*, which will get you disqualified—and then killed—before this whole thing even starts!"

"Why do you call me that?"

"Call you what?"

"Droo… whatever?"

"*Drummenir*. It means human." She shut her eyes and shook her head in despair. "It's not a nice way of saying it."

"… maybe you should stop using it, then?"

"I will say whatever I please. Unfortunately for me, I'm bound to your service, but the rules say nothing about how I should speak to you."

I took a deep breath to try and calm myself. It helped, but only a little. "Alright," I said, "I think you're unravelling, here. And *lucky* for you, I know a thing or two about panic attacks."

"I am *not* having a panic attack."

"Really? Because it looks like you're having trouble holding it together there. In fact, I'm the one being threatened with death, and you're more worked up than I am."

"I don't think the shock has set in yet," Gullie put in.

"Probably not. The point is, we're both in a bit of a situation, here."

"A situation? No, no, no. A wardrobe malfunction is a *situation*," Mira said, her eyes wide and wild. "You're facing death, while I'm facing a huge, personal disgrace. Which do you think is worse?"

"Death," Gullie and I said at the same time.

"Definitely my death," I added. "I think you need to work on your priorities."

"I need to tell someone about this. Maybe if I told them, fate won't punish me. Telling them is the right thing to do."

She started marching toward the door. I jumped into her path and intercepted her before she could reach it. "Wait, no, that's a bad, bad idea," I said, "Terrible idea."

"Why?" she asked.

"Because if you tell them, I'll tell them you tried to help me escape."

Mira scowled and folded her arms across her chest. "They'll never believe you."

"Do you want to bet on that?"

She stared at me, and I could see the gears working in her mind. Mira was trying to figure out if her people, the Unseelie fae of the *Winter Court*, would decide that what I was saying warranted verifying, or if they'd take the easiest and quietest approach, and just kill us both.

Mira screwed up her face and let out a frustrated huff. "This changes nothing," she hissed, "Your trials begin tomorrow, and you're going to fail."

"Probably, but what if I don't?"

She scoffed. "Do you have any idea who you're going up against?"

"I don't… and that means you have until tomorrow to train me."

"Me? Why me?"

"Because you've been sworn to help me succeed. Imagine what the Winter Court will do for you if I win. I don't think it's a long shot to say I'll probably have been the first ever human to win; a human with no training or experience. They'll give you everything you want."

She narrowed her eyes. "If I let you begin the trials knowing what you are, and they find out, they'll kill us both anyway."

"Sounds to me like we'd better get started."

Mira frowned. I was starting to think she hated all of this more than I did, and I was the one who'd been kidnapped. I could tell, though, that she was the kind of girl who didn't easily give up on her own goals and ambitions. She frowned and cocked her head to the side, lightly touching the corner of her mouth with a fingertip.

"I'm not convinced the Winter Court will give me everything I want if you win, but first things first, we're going to have to do something about…" she gestured up and down my body, "All of *this*."

I crossed my arms in front of my chest. "All of what?"

"You're going to meet the Prince tonight, and I'd sooner die than let *my ward* meet him looking like that."

"The Prince…"

"That's right."

"I'm meeting the *Prince*."

She frowned at me. "Are you having trouble understanding me?"

I wasn't. I also didn't want to go anywhere near the Prince, but that didn't seem like an option, not if I wanted to survive my time in this strange world and have any hopes of going back home.

Chapter Nine

I twirled in front of the mirror, examining myself in the fading light of the setting, Arcadian sun. I looked good, fitter than usual, shapelier than usual. My bum was round, my hips nicely curved, and my tits... I had *tits*, and Mira hadn't even begun laying a glamor on me.

That was all me.

I'd spent most of my adult life making my own clothes, realizing only now I'd never made anything that enhanced my natural feminine qualities. Don't get me wrong, my clothes were always perfectly fitted to my body, but I went for comfort and warmth over aesthetics.

Mira had brought me a snug, black dress that clung to me like a second skin, giving me a silhouette that was new, and strange, and *empowering*. I kind of liked it, and that wasn't like me at all. Then again, who was I, really?

"Alright," Mira said, "And now, onto the last step."

"How does it work?" I asked.

"Lucky for you, one of the skills Custodians are required to learn is the art of the glamor. Pageantry is everything here, and even contestants who are about to take to the field of battle should do so looking their best. Like I said earlier, a little showmanship will only boost your chances of succeeding; the same goes for makeup."

"So, do I tell you what I want, or?"

"You're in no position to tell me what looks good. Now, hush, and let me do my work."

Mira stepped up behind me and pulled my dull, brown hair into her hands. She started smoothing it slowly, running it between her fingers, always keeping one eye on the mirror in front of us. Her hands started glowing with soft, silvery light, and all along her arms tattoos were starting to appear like they were coming up from under her skin.

The tattoos stretching across Mira's arms were little more than lines at first, but they seemed to be following a kind of floral pattern that reached her shoulders. They were beautiful, delicate, and strange. Then the changes to my appearance took shape, and that… that was something else.

They came gently, but all at the same time; the most noticeable being my hair. It went from mousy brown and a little ratty, to wavy, cascading curls, deep grey at the top transitioning into sparkling silver strands.

My skin, once pale and pasty, remained pale, but was given a healthy glow that made me look younger, and more vibrant. I never usually wore too much makeup, but Mira gave me just enough to enhance what was already there instead of darkening my features like I normally would.

She stretched the tips of my ears into points, gave my lips a little more fullness, and made my canines turn into little fangs that felt weird in my mouth. But my eyes… she didn't touch my eyes. They remained mine, teal and bright, and twinkling against what was left of the sunlight.

When she was done, she pulled her hands away and moved around me, checking me out with her own eyes. "Better," she said, happy with her work. "There's still a little too much *drummenir* in you, but it's a start. With any luck, he won't be entirely repulsed."

I shook my head at her. "You aren't very nice, does anyone ever tell you that?"

She glanced at my reflection. "No, because they aren't very nice either, so they don't care. Now, here are the rules." Mira ushered me toward the door. "You are to speak—"

"—only when spoken to, etcetera, etcetera. I know."

"Good, but let's add a few more rules to that list. First, if your harpy insists on hiding in your hair, ensure she isn't seen."

"I'm a *pixie*, not a harpy," Gullie grumbled.

Secondly," Mira continued, "Keep your sentences short and to the point. Nobody likes a rambler. And third, keep your hands off the Prince. You aren't a Royal, and therefore it is forbidden for you to touch him."

"Why would I—"

Mira cocked a perfect eyebrow at me, and I understood. He was gorgeous. People probably wanted to touch him all the time. "Right," I said. "Got it."

Shaking her head, she opened the door and led me down the same corridor I'd been through earlier. Instead of heading for the great hall, though, she took me through a series of long hallways, some of which were wide, and open, and outdoors, where the air was crisp and cold.

Fae cliques meandered around, some gathered in the courtyard, others moving up and down the same walkways I was going through. Every last one of them stared at me and hushed as I walked past them, making me wonder if they could tell I was really human underneath Mira's glamor. In truth, I didn't know how glamors worked, but I doubted if Mira would be walking so close to me if she thought my humanness could be uncovered with a glance.

I lost my bearings after a while, confused by the many hallways and corridors I was moving through. They all looked the same, and this place was immense, almost to the point where I wondered if they'd ever considered installing a public transit system to make getting around easier, and quicker.

Mira eventually brought me to a door being watched over by two guards carrying swords at their sides. The door opened as we reached it, and a girl came out wearing the exact same black dress I was wearing. She hurried out of the room, not making eye contact with anyone as she rushed past.

"What happened to her?" I asked, keeping my voice low.

"The Prince is an… intense kind of man. Not everyone can handle it, but you must if you want to make a good impression."

"Do I?"

"If you want to last long in these trials, you do. Not that I have any faith in you. Now, go. Don't keep him waiting."

My heart lurched into my throat and started thumping hard, making it incredibly difficult to walk into the room with any grace. If the Prince was a wolf in his den, I was starting to feel like I was stumbling into it wearing a bleeding meat-suit.

Beyond the doors was a spacious, white room lit by fireflies trapped in glass balls. The light they gave off was soft, amber, and warm. As the light orbs moved within their baubles, the ambience in the room shifted, simulating something like firelight. At the center of the room was a series of long, luxuriant couches, and on a round table between them, two sparkling glasses filled with a pale, blue liquid.

I hadn't noticed the Prince until he stepped off the open-air balcony at the far end of the room and moved into view. Holy hell, he was huge. Even from a distance, he was already bigger than me, and the closer he got, the larger he loomed, the more intense his almost predatory aura seemed to get. I found myself already shrinking away from him, but as soon as I caught myself, I held my ground.

I'm not about to be chased off like that other girl.

Just as I finished the thought, the Prince stopped dead in his tracks. He slid one of his hands out of his pockets and ran it through his black beard, watching me from where he stood. It wasn't so much shock or surprise, but it did look something like mental preparation. I wasn't sure what part of him to look at; his ice blue eyes, his strong, full lips, or the antlers curling around his temples.

I decided not to make eye contact at all if I could help it, remembering how I'd had to rip my eyes away from him last time, and just how difficult that had been.

"You look different," he said, his words rolling over my skin.

"I had a chance to clean up," I said, reminding myself that, here, I was fae—not human. "Your Highness…"

A pause. "I trust your accommodations are to your satisfaction?"

"They are, though I wish I'd been given a pamphlet or something to read before having been brought here."

"A pamphlet?" He seemed genuinely confused by the word.

"You know, something to provide a little context as to why I had been ripped from my home at sword-point."

"You were already late for the reception. There was no time to brief you." He paused just as he arrived with the glass in his hand. "Why didn't your parents brief you?"

I turned my gaze up at him, now, daring to lock eyes with the Prince of this strange realm. It was a mistake. A huge mistake. Prince Cillian was easily the most well put-together man in existence. All fae were beautiful, and graceful, but he was several levels above even that. He was beauty, and grace, and masculinity, wrapped in an aura of predatory lethality that intimidated me as much as it excited me.

Even with two dainty wine glasses in his hands, he looked ready. Ready to turn them into weapons. Ready to lay low anyone who would dare lift a finger against him. And I was about to lie to him.

"They were busy," I said.

"Busy?"

"That's right. Don't your people also get busy?"

"We do… but the Royal Selection is one of the greatest honors a young fae might receive—especially if you win. I'm surprised you weren't expecting us."

"Really? Fighting each other on a battlefield for the privilege of marrying a Prince is one of the greatest honors we can receive?"

"You disagree."

"I do. Strongly."

He narrowed his eyes. "It's no wonder you're so clearly unprepared for the trials ahead." He handed one of the glasses over. "But you are here now. Drink with me," he said, and I saw the sharpened canines behind his lips, further emphasizing what I already felt about him, the fear, the fascination… the attraction.

A cross between elk, human, and wolf, brought to life with magic.

I took the glass, because to refuse him would mean… well, it probably wouldn't have been good to refuse his offer. But I didn't drink. Not only did I distrust the contents of that blue liquid that smelled strangely like frozen berries, but I had never sipped from a glass handed to me by a stranger before, and I wasn't about to start now.

"To the Royal Selection," he said, raising his own glass.

I raised mine in return, brought it to my lips, but I didn't join him in taking a sip.

The Prince's mouth turned into an amused, half-smile. "Do you know it is a crime to refuse a toast from a Prince?" he asked, lowering his glass.

"Kidnapping is also a crime where I'm from," I said.

"Kidnapping is a crime in most places, but we did no such thing. You are from here, you *belong* here."

I was about to keep pushing, I wanted to keep pushing, but these people thought I was someone else. If I asked too many questions, if I made him start doubting himself, I ran the risk of making my already flimsy cover unravel.

What I needed to do was try and learn more about who they thought I was. Someone had made a mistake when they targeted me for retrieval, and I had to know who that was and why they'd made that mistake.

"Your castle is impressive," I said, stepping away from him—away from the heat his body radiated—and heading toward the balcony.

"I don't want to talk about my castle," he said, "I want to talk about you, *Dahlia*…"

The sound of my name on his lips sent an electric current racing into the base of my spine and back up again. I swallowed hard, then glanced at him from across my shoulder.

"Don't you know all you need to know about me already?" I asked.

"I know your name," he said, following me, "I know you were chosen to take part in these trials."

"I'm surprised you don't know more."

"It is against the rules for me to know more about the participants of the Royal Selection before it begins."

"You follow rules?"

His eyes narrowed. "More than you know, but I don't expect you to believe that. Tell me a little more about yourself. For example, what were you doing at that mage's house?"

I paused, watching him as he approached. "How about you answer that question for me? You were there, too."

"I don't have to discuss crown secrets with you."

"Then I don't have to discuss mine, either."

The Prince's eyes narrowed, but I noticed the slightest curling of his lips. "You're not used to being around royalty, are you?"

"Used to it? No. Not really. What gave it away?"

"I'm sure I could name a couple of things. You still haven't joined me in my toast, for example."

I glanced at the bright, blue liquid in the long-necked glass. "I make it a point not to accept drinks from strangers."

"So as to avoid poisons. I see your point."

"Poisons? Well, yes, I suppose you could call them poisons."

"But I am a Prince, not a commoner."

"In my experience, it's the wealthy ones that are more likely to try to *poison* you."

"Intriguing." He trailed off. "You certainly don't behave in the manner that is expected, you aren't prepared for the trials, and you seem to know nothing of your homeland. Perhaps that is why I find you so intriguing, Dahlia."

Intriguing? And there's my name again. My skin tingled. "I don't like being someone else's entertainment."

"The Royal Selection is entertainment for the court, but for me it is much more than that."

"Is it? Because you seem pretty amused most of the time."

He turned his head to the side. "Believe me, I have dreaded this day for a long time. I find this entire thing boring beyond belief."

"I find that really hard to believe."

"Believe what you like, but I am telling you the truth. Your fellow competitors have practiced for years to get to where they are today, but in that they are not alone. I have also been made to practice etiquette, to learn decorum, and refine my poise. That is all time that has taken away from more important duties. But then you came along."

"Me?"

"There is something about you. Something I cannot quite pinpoint."

Maybe that I'm human? "I wish I could help you figure that out, but I have to get ready for my first trial tomorrow. Unless you want to call this whole, boring thing off and send us all back home?"

He glanced at me again. "That, I cannot do, but I can wish you good fortunes. The competition will not be easy, and many will be watching closely. Most of them expect you to fail."

I rolled my eyes. "Of course. What about you?"

He cocked an eyebrow. "I have to agree with them."

"Well, that's rude."

The Prince raised his glass and pressed it lightly against his lips. "Prove us all wrong."

"Is that a challenge?"

He gave a little shrug, a playful smirk, and then he sipped his wine. "It is what you want it to be."

"That look probably gets you whatever you want, doesn't it?"

"Not everything I want."

"What's that supposed to mean?"

"It means, give me your hand."

I glanced at my hand, then turned my eyes back at him. "Why?"

"See? It doesn't get me everything I want. But I would like to see your hand."

My heart picked up the pace and started pumping against the sides of my neck. Hesitantly, I decided to do as he asked and give him my hand if only to keep him from noticing that I still hadn't dared drink from his glass.

The moment his skin touched mine, my heart started pounding against my ribs like a prisoner trapped inside of a cage. I almost couldn't breathe. His skin was so warm, his hands soft, but firm. He traced the lines along my palm with his fingertips, making my entire body tremble like a snowflake caught on a leaf.

"What—" I had to take a breath, "What are you doing?"

The carefully examined my hand. "Do you believe in fate?" he asked.

I frowned. "Fate?"

"Destiny. Serendipity. Chance."

"I know what the word means."

"Well?"

I watched his fingers as he delicately stroked my palm, trying my best to keep my composure from cracking apart like a brittle twig. "I've grown up with magic all around me."

"Of course, you have. But fate is bigger than magic. Fate is… cosmic. Primal. I believe it to be the single most ancient thing in existence."

"Older than Gods?"

"Gods are manifestations of fate as interpreted by the people who birth them."

"That's deep. Are you saying you don't believe in Gods?"

"I'm saying my belief in fate itself as a driving force behind all things is far stronger than my belief in Gods. Call me old-fashioned."

I almost asked him what he considered old-fashioned. I had no idea how old he was, but the fae lived for centuries—some were immortal, or so the rumors went. For all I knew, the Prince was a hundred years old. What was old-fashioned for a centenarian?

"I'm not sure where you're going with this," I said.

He brought his eyes up to meet mine, his gaze intense, and deep. "You were brought here for a reason, Dahlia. Fate itself has touched your life—all our lives. We can choose to fight it or embrace it."

I swallowed hard. "What… what are you going to do?"

His thumb reached my wrist, sending an electric jolt into my arm, followed by a trickle of excited warmth that reached my chest. "I haven't decided yet."

Belore.

That was the first word he had ever said to me. It flashed in my mind like a neon sign, flickering on and off, blinking rapidly. I didn't know what it meant, but I remembered seeing something like recognition in his eyes when he'd said it. I thought I saw a little more of that now, and it scared me enough to make me yank my hand away from his.

I had to, otherwise I thought I was going to collapse under the weight of his gaze.

It was too much, too intense, too *hot*. My heart was fluttering, my breaths had shortened, and I was starting to lose all feeling in my toes. I'd never been in the presence of a man quite as incredibly attractive as Prince Cillian, much less been the subject of such a man's scrutiny.

He tilted his head to the side and frowned. "Did I say something upsetting?" he asked.

"No… but I should go. I've used up way too much of your time."

Moving briskly over to the same table he was standing at, I set my glass down and went to head for the door, but he grabbed my hand and stopped me. I turned my head and gaped at him, my heart thundering. He looked like he was stuck between wanting to speak, and not knowing what to say.

I almost felt the same way he did. It was difficult to wrap my head around. I knew I had never met this man in my entire life, there was no way we could've possibly crossed paths. But the first time he'd touched me, I'd felt something deep within me start rising to the surface, and I felt it again now.

It wasn't like recognition, though; it didn't feel like familiarity, but it did feel like... like a connection, of some kind. Something deep, and ancient.

Something *destined*.

The Prince's grip on my hand loosened, and I took the opportunity to leave, in the end rushing out of the room just like that other girl had. I wondered if she'd left for the same reason as me; I wondered if she had felt the same things I had and been scared off by it.

No, this was unique.

This had caught him off guard just as much as it had frightened the hell out of me. The only question now was, what the hell had we felt, and how could I stop that from happening again?

Chapter Ten

Mira escorted me back to my room, but she didn't stick around; not that I would've let her, anyway. Not after what had just happened. I needed to be by myself for a while. I needed to process everything that had happened today, but more importantly, I needed to prepare myself.

Tonight was to be my first night spent in a fae castle.

There was only one consolation, one thing that made this train wreck of a day even remotely more… palatable. A lavish table had been prepared, completely with tablecloth and candles, near one of the large windows overlooking city, and the mountains off in the distance.

In front of the table was a comfortable dining chair, and on the table were a series of platters with silver domes on them. A pitcher of clear, clean water sat next to the domed plates, accompanied by another pitcher filled with luminous, blue wine; the same wine the Prince had been drinking.

A warm, homely, mouth-watering scent filled the air, and for the first time since I'd been here, I didn't feel like my life was in imminent danger.

Unless the fae poisoned the food?

Gullie zipped out of my hair and hovered over to the table. "Wow!" she gasped, "Look at all this stuff!"

I hovered over to the table, slowly, carefully, despite my roaring stomach. I hadn't eaten a proper meal since breakfast, and everything smelled so good in here all I wanted to do was tear those silver domes off and tuck into whatever was underneath them. There were so many plates, plates of all sizes, it looked like a feast had been set up just for me.

"Gull…" I said.

Gullie turned around to look at me and hovered in mid-air. "Yeah?"

"You know the fae pretty well, right?"

"Not pretty well, no. I mean, I know them a little. Why?"

I reached the table and ran my fingertips along the white tablecloth. "Because… I mean, this is food, isn't it? Under these domes?"

"Did you hit your head or something? Of course, it's food!"

"How likely is it any of this is poisoned?"

Gullie gave me a look like I was talking utter nonsense. "You're kidding me, right?"

"Well, I don't know, do I?!"

She gestured to the largest of the silver domes. "How about you lift one and find out?"

As I scanned the table, I couldn't help but catch a glimpse of the city of Windhelm as it rolled away from my window. It was a breathtakingly beautiful maze of sparkling ice walls and homes lit by thousands, and thousands of torches that went almost as far as the eye could see.

Some of the streets were alive with shifting, glowing light of different colors. Even from up here I could see movement on some of the parapets and towers furthest away from the castle. The long, thin bridge that connected the city to the mainland like a neck covered in jewels glimmered against the night, carts ferrying back and forth across it.

"Wow…" I sighed, echoing Gullie's sentiment from before.

She came up beside me, her little body taking my attention away from the city and putting it firmly back on me. I didn't recognize myself with this hair, these long ears, this makeup. I didn't know who the girl in the mirror was, but it wasn't me. It couldn't be me. The real me was waiting back at home, desperate for me to come back.

"I have to hand it to them," Gullie said, "The fae really do know how to build cities."

My vision focused on the city again, then my stomach rumbled, and my eyes lowered to the spread on the table in front of me. "Alright... I'm too hungry to care whether this is poison or not. Shall we have a look?"

Gullie zipped down to the table, her green form racing across the silver domes. I reached for the largest one, grabbed hold of the top, and picked it up. A breath of steam issued out from under it, warming my cold face. The heady aroma that followed, though, made the rumbling in my stomach almost unbearable.

On the plate was an assortment of meat, roasted potatoes, and colorful vegetables that didn't look all too different from what I might find at home. I wasn't sure if the fae bred chickens out here, but whatever was on the plate sure smelled like chicken. Immediately I sat down on the chair as if it had pulled me to it.

"Oh my God..." Gullie said, "That looks amazing."

"And there's more," I said, picking up silver domes and setting them aside.

There was a gravy boat to go with my food, a stick of butter, some bread, a bowl of fruits that kind of looked like grapes, if grapes could glow, and a steaming pie that looked way too big for me to eat by myself. I was sure as hell going to try, though, especially after the day I'd had.

Surveying the table, I picked the bread up, set it down next to the butter, and then on the small plate where the bread had been, I set a small portion of food for Gullie to eat. Pixies didn't eat much, but for their size, they had crazy appetites, so I made sure to give her plenty of food to eat... and then I ate.

And I ate.

And I ate.

To be clear, I stuffed my face. We both did. We didn't touch the wine, though; we drank only water. But by the time we were done, really done, there were only remnants of the feast left. Gullie was on her back, rubbing her stomach and staring at the ceiling. I was just about ready to slip into a food coma after everything I'd just eaten.

"Is this what they're feeding all the participants?" I asked.

"They probably expect you to carb up before the competition really begins," Gullie said, then she burped. "Oops… sorry."

"*Manners*, Gull."

"Hey, I said sorry. I could get used to this you know."

"Don't get used to it. We *can't* get too used to it."

"I said I *could…* not that I will." She paused. "So, do you want to talk about what happened with the Prince?"

"I don't know. It was a lot. This whole thing has been a lot, and he's just… the cherry on top."

"Cherry?"

I shook my head. "Alright, no, cherry was the wrong analogy."

Gullie pointed at the bowl of grapes, still mostly full. They'd been deliciously sweet, but they were frozen solid. I had to warm them on my tongue before I could bite into them. "He's more like those grapes... cold and hard on the outside, but you know what?"

I frowned. "What?"

"He's probably also cold and hard on the inside."

"They were so good in that pie, though."

"So, we stick him in a pie. Maybe that'll make him taste nice, too."

"I don't want to taste him, Gull."

She turned her little pixie head and looked up at me, her eyebrows wagging. "You *sure*?"

I frowned. "Don't be silly. That man is the furthest thing on my mind right now."

Okay, that wasn't strictly true. I was trying to convince myself as well as Gullie, and I knew it. The only problem was, I'd never been a great liar. I remembered having walked into the kitchen one day, following the heady aroma of baked goods, to find a huge spread of cookies and pies laid out. It looked like a bakery had exploded all over the kitchen, and it smelled like there were more in the oven.

I didn't think anyone would notice, so I went around the room, sampling cookies and pies like a connoisseur, and once I'd had my fill, I left. Later, when mother Pepper accused mother Evie of having dipped her hand in the metaphorical cookie jar—her sweet tooth was as strong as mine—I cracked without even being the prime suspect.

So, as much as I wanted to believe the Prince didn't feature anywhere in my thoughts, it just wasn't true. He was there, and so were his winter-blue eyes, those full lips, those round shoulders—and that voice. I took a deep breath and exhaled. His voice, though strong, and authoritative, carried hidden softness to it I didn't think the fae around here had ever noticed, or even cared to notice.

Hearing my name roll off his tongue did things to my body that hadn't been done to me for a long time, if they'd ever been done to me at all. I couldn't very well tell *her* that, though; otherwise she would never let it go, and I didn't have the energy to deal with that kind of thing right now.

I let my head fall against the backrest of the large dining chair I'd been sitting on and sighed. "I want to go home, Gull," I said.

"I know… I don't like it here, either. You weren't made for this."

I rolled my eyes. "*Cheers*, Gullie."

"No, I just mean—pixies are born into a pretty harsh world. The fae destroyed all of our homelands long, long ago because they're jerks and they hate us, so my people move around a lot. When you're a society of travelers and nomads, if you can't keep up with the convoy, you get left behind."

I sat upright again and looked at the little pixie, still laying on her back on the table. "How did I not know this already?"

"I don't like talking about things that make me sad, but I'm making an exception right now to put the point across that… I'm a competitor. I have been since birth, and that's not a bad thing. I just think, this is literally the worst place you could've been forced to come to."

"I'm competitive…" I said, a little meekly.

Gullie stood up and walked to the edge of the table. "I'm saying this because I love you, Dee. Your mothers have kept you very tightly wrapped up. You've never wanted for anything, you've never lacked anything, you've never needed anything so desperately you had to make hard choices to try and get it. I mean, you just went on your first delivery, *just* now. They haven't given you enough independence, and now we're here, and the last thing I want is to see you get hurt, but I'm so freaking worried."

I gave her a bemused look. "I think you're more fae than you think."

She frowned. "Why?"

"Because in a roundabout way, you just told me I'm too soft to be here."

"I've never lied to you once. I'm not gonna start now. But I will promise you… *re*-promise you… wherever you go, I'll be there. Whatever you need, I'll give it to you. And if you go down, I go down with you."

I shook my head. "That's stupid. You can't do that. If something happens to me, you have to flee."

"And go where? Arcadia isn't my home anymore. Anyway, I'll freeze out there on my own just like you would." She held out the tiniest pinkie. "Pinkie promise."

A slight smile tugged at the corner of my mouth. I offered her my pinkie, and since we couldn't entwine them, she tapped mine with hers. "Then I'm going to fight like I've never fought before," I said. "Pinkie promise."

Smiling, Gullie nodded, then she took to the air leaving a glittering trail of pixie dust to fall around the plates on the table. "How about we go check out that bed?" she asked, "I don't know about you, but I'm exhausted."

I turned my head and glanced at the massive, plush looking bed that was covered in furry rugs. "I'm pretty tired too," I said, "I'm dreading trying to get to sleep in here, though."

"Why?"

"I've never slept outside of home before. I don't think I'll be able to get any sleep."

She floated over to my face, grinning. "Good thing you have *me* to help you sleep." Gullie cupped her hand, and a little cloud of green, sparkling mist began to writhe and move between her fingertips. "C'mon, you'll be fine. Besides, you need your rest. The real fun begins tomorrow."

Chapter Eleven

I awoke to what sounded like church-bells gonging in the distance. The bells were far enough away that the noise didn't wake me up with a start. I was slow to rouse, sluggish because I had slept so comfortably, so completely. Despite the room looking like it was made of solid ice, the bed itself had been plush, and warm, the sheets silken, the covers furry.

I didn't want to get up.

I didn't want to leave the bed.

But Mira had other plans. Barely a few minutes after waking, Mira entered my room without knocking and came marching over to the bed. I sat upright, pulling the covers up to my chest. With a harsh look and a flash of her eyes, she warned me to make sure Gullie wasn't seen, so I made sure the pixie was tucked away under the covers while a contingent of people entered the room to clear last night's dinner and deliver today's breakfast.

"Oh my God," Gullie whispered. "Is that food?"

"Yes," I said into the sheets.

"It smells so good… like living in a French bakery."

"I know. I'm still full from last night, though. I don't know if I could eat."

"Yeah, and you don't want to go through your first trail on a full stomach. I should eat the food for you. You know, to wipe away the temptation."

"I doubt even you could finish what they're bringing in. It looks like another feast."

One by one, servants brought in platter after platter of food, as well as a pitcher of water, and another filled with some kind of teal colored juice that looked like it had fruity pulp floating around inside. When they were gone, I pulled the blanket back to let Gullie out, then I wrapped it around myself and sat on the edge of the bed.

"Is this going to happen every morning?" I asked.

"Correct," Mira said, "As soon as the bells chime the start of the morning."

Gullie streamed over to the table to start inspecting what had been delivered. I decided to leave her to it—I really was still too full to even consider eating. Anyway, my upcoming trial had my stomach in knots. I doubted if I could swallow even a single bite, no matter how delicious it all smelled.

"So, what's on the agenda?" I asked.

Mira crossed the bedroom to the bathroom, beckoning me to follow her. As soon as we walked inside, soft, white lights bloomed to illuminate the room. With a flick of her wrist, a plug keeping water from flooding into the bathtub popped out of its place, allowing it to start filling up. She then picked up a small, ornate looking bottle, opened the top, and poured some of the blue liquid inside into the water, creating big, foamy bubbles.

"Bath, first," Mira said. "I want you to look your absolute best today in front of the court, but more importantly, I need you to *smell* your best."

"Yeah, people keep saying I stink," I said, "And that's just rude."

"Take it personally. It's intended that way." She clapped her hands. "Now, let's do this quickly. We don't have a lot of time."

I put my finger up to ask her a question, but she was already on the move, so I didn't. Instead, I stared at the bath for some time, watching the water bubble in the white tub, unsure about disrobing in a castle that looked like it was made of ice. Would I freeze?

As soon as I noticed the fingers of steam rising from the waterline, I made the decision to quickly disrobe and lower myself into the tub. The water was blissfully warm, and it smelled flowery, and luxuriant.

For a while, I forgot where I was. I would've fallen asleep inside the tub, staring up at the skylight above, if not for Mira. It was as if I could hear her impatience growing, and growing, and growing. When she'd had enough of waiting, she entered the bathroom again holding a large robe and a fresh change of clothes, setting it all down on a small stool near the tub without saying a word.

I emerged from the washroom once I'd changed to find her setting things down on the bed. First, I spotted the sword and the dagger, gorgeous, sharp, and dangerous. Beside them was a black outfit that looked tough and sturdy, like it was made of leather. But some of the pieces had metal plates on them, and that made me worry a little.

"You weren't kidding about the army thing, were you?" I asked.

"I'm sorry?" Mira asked.

"At the announcement. The voice said the winner of the Royal Selection would lead an army. I guess that means the women I'm going up against know how to fight? I take it that's what all this is for?"

Mira's lips pressed into a thin line. She nodded. "Yes. Like I said, they have been training for ten years, and not just in the art of combat, but in everything. They know how to behave like royalty, they know how to fight like royalty, and they know *magic*."

"Uh, *like royalty*," Gullie put in, mimicking Mira's voice, and earning one hell of a scowl.

"Well," I started checking things off with my fingers, "I can't fight, I certainly can't do any magic, I haven't *run* anywhere in years, and I'm a painfully awkward person when it comes to social encounters. Like, catastrophically awkward. So, no. You don't have to remind me. What you have to do, is find a way to make me even halfway decent."

She shook her head. "As I was retrieving these items, I found myself thinking just what a pointless endeavor this is."

I cocked a thumbs up at her. "Cheers for the encouragement."

"But then I decided, how hard can it be for us to get out of this mess?"

"Not the direction I thought you were going with that."

Mira walked over to me. "Think about it. All we have to do is make you look convincing. If you die during your trials, well, at least I won't find myself disgraced. I can try again. This isn't the first Royal Selection, and it won't be the last."

"That's…" I pinched the bridge of my nose and shook her head at how casual she'd made that all sound. "Don't the King and Queen need to have another child of age before another Royal Selection can happen? I'm just guessing here, but we also have a Monarchy where I come from, and yours probably isn't that different to mine."

Her eyes brightened. "You have a Monarchy also? *Really*?"

"You didn't know that?"

"I don't know much about the human world. What I do know is that you're all uncultured, uncivilized, stinking savages with absolutely no prospects of ever becoming more than fertilizer for the next batch of humans."

I stared at her, my eyebrows arched *way* high. "Charming," I said. "Where I'm from, we're told the fae are all cruel, ruthless jerks with no sense of morals and no issues with murder if it serves to further an agenda. And that's what they say about the *Seelie fae*; don't get me started with you Unseelie types."

She waved her hand. "Preposterous. And I don't understand your need to divide us into Seelie and Unseelie. Those are human concepts and labels put on our kind. Winter, Summer, Autumn, Spring, the truth is we're all capable of great good as well as great evil… we simply go about our endeavors in a more sophisticated manner than you humans do. But you have a Monarchy! That means the stories can't all be true, can they? What are your Royals like? Do all humans serve them? Do they know magic, also?"

"I'd love to sit here and talk about the Queen of England with you, but I feel like we're getting off topic. You need to be training me."

"*Or*, I can make you look like one of the fae, send you off into your trials, and you can do me the favor of dying with a little showmanship? The crowd will love that. And… then I can at least go back to my life."

Already I could feel *desperation* filling me, but I pressed on. "I want to go home too, you know. I don't want to die here. I'm only taking part in this thing because I need to survive long enough for my mothers to find me."

"Mothers?" she asked, frowning. "You have more than one?"

"I have three. It's a long story. But they're mages, powerful mages, and when they find out I've been taken, they're going to come looking for me."

Mira looked at me like I'd just spoken to her in three different languages. "You have more than one mother, and they are all *verenir*… and yet you are *drummenir*. I don't understand how that works."

I pointed a finger at her. "Okay, I don't know what *verenir* means, but I'm going to assume it's a derogatory term for mage. Please don't use those words anymore. You don't need to insult me or my people."

The beautiful fae frowned. "Very well," she said. "It's the least I can do, considering you'll probably die. Your mothers will, also, if they attempt to reclaim you. Windhelm is an impenetrable fortress that has stood for ten thousand years, and Arcadia herself may only be entered with permission, and escort, from a Royal fae. I can assure you; your mothers will not be able to reach you here."

So, that's why the Prince was there. The soldiers he was with couldn't have come to the human world on their own—he was their Royal escort. But he'd been on his way to Madame Whitmore's Academy when we bumped into each other, I was sure of it. He'd made a pit-stop before picking me up, and that meant he had business in the human world. Possibly regular business. All I had to do was stowaway with him the next time he went on another kidnapping trip to Earth.

Great, because stealth is yet another one of your strong suits.

"Then I have to get the Prince to send me back," I said, "Fat chance of that if last night was any indication, but still, I can try."

"And how do you suppose you'll convince him to take you back? Prince Cillian isn't exactly known for his generosity… or his kindness; or his empathy, for that matter. It's why he's such a desirable Prince."

I paused and stared at her, wondering whether I should tell her what had happened last night—what I thought had passed between me and the Prince. Maybe she had some insight she could give me, or advice.

Maybe she knew what that word meant.

Belore.

That's what she was here for, at the end of the day; to give me advice and steer me in the right direction. In the end, though, it came down to trust. I didn't think I could trust her, not even after all she had said last night.

The fae were notorious tricksters and liars, after all.

"What can you tell me about the Prince?" I asked.

"You didn't learn much during your talk last night, I gather?"

"Not really, but he didn't exactly strike me as the kind of man to look favorably on charity cases like mine."

"He isn't that kind of person, no. As I said before, he's not known for being very generous. He has an impressive record, however."

"Record?"

"He is the youngest knight in the Winter Court, he has never been defeated in combat, and he is the only living Winter Court fae in all of Windhelm to have braved the scorching desert at the height of summer and come back alive to talk about it. Legend has it that, as a boy, his father would take him hunting for giants. After, they would drink the giant's blood and become stronger for it."

"That sounds gross… and also insane. Giants?" I shook my head.

"Oh, yes. The frost giants of the north. They don't normally come very close to Windhelm, but lately there have been more and more sightings."

"And the royals go hunting for them?"

"Of course, giants are considered undesirables among our kind. They know they aren't to step within our borders, but some do so anyway. That makes them fair game."

"I don't know how I feel about that."

"You'll have to feel the same way we do, I'm afraid. As a General in our army, you may have to someday repel our borders against them."

"Let's not get ahead of ourselves; I won't make it that far if I'm dead. How about you tell me what I'm in for?"

"Well," Mira said, walking around the room. "This morning there will be a ceremony, followed by your first trial; a simple test of physical prowess."

I looked at my hands, trailing my eyes up and along my—lack of—biceps. "Physical prowess?" I asked.

"Oh, yes. You must be able to hold your own in battle against any number of foes. Success here will give you a good start in the trials that follow."

I walked over to the sword and the dagger sitting on the desk. "I've never so much as thrown a rock in my life, let alone stabbed someone."

The weapons were beautiful, and sleek. Their handles were made of leather, which probably made them easier to swing around. Turquoise gems were set into their silver cross-guards, but the blades themselves didn't look metallic—they were different shades of blue that went from dark at the hilt, to light at the tip.

Like hard ice.

I picked the sword up, and instantly regretted it. "Holy hell, that thing is heavy."

Mira walked over to me, grabbed the dagger, and placed it in my hand. "Then, in that case, you'll use a dagger. But make no mistake, you won't be stabbing anyone."

"I won't?"

"Do you think you could stab me?"

I cocked an eyebrow. "I'm holding a dagger, aren't I?"

She smiled at me, but it was an evil, mischievous kind of smile. "Then stab me."

I didn't want to stab her, but then I thought about how much of an *arse* she'd been, and that was enough to make me thrust the dagger at her. She twirled out of its path effortlessly, like she was made of water. Then she grabbed my arm, twisted it behind my back, knocked the dagger out of my hand, and pushed me up against the desk.

"What the hell?" I yelped.

A pause, then Mira let me go. "You're *absolutely* going to die," she said, shaking her head. "I've disarmed you, and I haven't trained nearly as long as they have."

I rubbed my aching hand. "Okay, fine. But I'm quick? Maybe I can avoid getting hit. Do you know which one of them I'll be fighting?"

"I don't. I don't even know if it will be one of them you'll be fighting. I only know the first trial is a physical one. Do you have any athletic skills?"

"I mean… I've never gone to a gym, but I've spent my fair share of afternoons evading bullies?"

"Evasion, then, will be your tactic. I'll teach you how to move like water. Maybe you'll learn, maybe you won't. With any luck, you'll die quickly. With *exceptional* luck, you'll advance to the next round. Either way, I'm comfortable with the way this is going."

I rolled my eyes. "Yeah, I mean, what else would you be doing tonight, right?"

"Exactly," she beamed. "See? Now you're getting it."

"The fae don't really understand sarcasm, do you?"

"Sweetie, we *invented* sarcasm. Now, let's figure out how to make you not suck at this… for your sakes. Your harpy is going to help."

"*Pixie*," Gullie snapped from inside my hair, "And I can't help. The moment I make myself known, we're both dead."

"So, don't make yourself known. But without your magic, I don't see how she'll get past her trials."

"That's a lot of pressure for a pixie to be under."

"Don't worry," I said, "I'm not going to let them find you, I promise. I don't want you to do anything, just be there with me… and if anything happens, get away as fast as you can."

"I won't leave your side."

Smiling, I picked my dagger up from the floor and held it in my hand, getting used to the weight, the feel of it. I looked up at Mira. "Alright," I said, "Let's do this."

Chapter Twelve

I had never worn leather before, let alone leather armor, but I was wearing the hell out of this outfit today.

Sliding my hand into black gloves lined with small metal plates made me feel strangely powerful. Like I could slam my fist into a wall and knock it down. I wasn't going to put that to the test, but the feeling was there all the same.

The black leather corset and pants were surprisingly lightweight, but they looked like they could take the sting out of a blow with a lead pipe. And the gloves on my hands went all the way up to my elbow, the leather pads there also lined with metal plates sturdy enough that they could probably stop a sword, if I was strong enough to block it.

What the hell am I thinking? I'm not blocking any swords with these twig arms.

Heading down to the grand hall, where the Royal Selection was due to start, I thought about all the stories I'd been told about how fae and humans interacted. It was never good. If mages snubbed their noses at humans, and the fae looked down on even mages, that put my kind way down at the bottom of the totem pole.

It wasn't that they were inherently better or stronger than mages, or werewolves, or even vampires; the fae just liked thinking they were. At least, that was the rumor. They were conceited, snobbish, and intolerant of others who weren't like them. They didn't particularly like their own kind, either—especially not from one Court to another.

It was a wonder they had any kind of civilization at all, with prejudices like those.

In one thing, though, they were always united; and that was their utter contempt for humans. I'd always heard rumors about what happened to humans who were stolen away to Arcadia. Almost all those stories ended with the human never returning home; either because they were trapped here, because the fae had killed them, or because they'd forgotten who they were, where they came from, and ended up transforming into strange, Arcadian monsters.

I had to make sure that didn't happen to me.

I had to remember where I was from, and what I was fighting for.

As I set foot in the grand hall where I'd made my humiliating entrance into the Winter Court, I couldn't help but notice how it had changed. The stands and stalls leading up to the royal balcony were gone, turned instead into a completely rounded coliseum-type area surrounded by tall walls. At the center of the coliseum, five other women stood around a large platform, and on the platform was a huge, sky blue gemstone wreathed in bright, white fire and fairy lights.

The gemstone hummed with magic and power, so much so that I could feel it vibrating against my bones.

Approaching the platform, I noticed the women were all wearing outfits that were identical to mine; black straps of finely crafted leather. Yet, naturally, they made it look way better than I did. The light from the gem hit bodies in fantastic ways, enhancing the color of their glowing eyes, their vibrant hair, their various bits of jewelry. They were all staring at it directly, almost in reverence.

Then I saw the weapons they were carrying; that was the point where my heart started to pound, as the reality of what was about to happen hit me fully.

"This is where I leave you," Mira said.

"You can't," I whispered between my teeth, "I don't know what the hell I'm doing out here."

"I trained you as much as I could, the rest is up to you."

"Mira!" I hissed, but she'd already started walking away. For a moment I stayed rooted to the spot, frozen, unable to approach the gemstone.

"You need to move," Gullie whispered, "Otherwise they might just kill you right now."

"I…" stammering, trying to move my lips as little as possible. "I don't know if I can."

Gullie pinched the back of my neck, and I could've swatted her out of my hair, but I didn't. Instead, I started walking toward what looked like an open space around the gemstone at the center of the coliseum. None of the fae nearby turned to look at me, or even registered my presence. They were just staring up at the heart of the gem, their eyes wide and glowing.

It looked like they were in a trance; *not quite all there*.

Then I felt it. It was like someone had thrown a lasso around my brain and tugged hard. I shut my eyes and ground my teeth, fighting the sensation, but the power was immense, and way more than I could resist. Eventually, it took hold of me. My eyes shot open on their own, and all I could see was white in front of me.

"State your name," came a soft, feminine voice. I heard it between my ears, like I was wearing earbuds.

"My… name," I said, despite my best efforts at keeping quiet, "My name is Dahlia Crowe."

"Dahlia Crowe, you have been brought here, to the great hall of Windhelm, to participate in the Royal Selection. In order to succeed, you must face several trials to prove you are worthy of the honors that shall be bestowed upon you. Should you be successful, glory unimaginable shall be yours… but it is possible you will meet your death in this place. Do you understand?"

"I understand."

"Do you submit, willingly, to abide by the rules of the Royal Selection, and deliver to us the best of your abilities throughout this competition?"

A pause. I could think for myself, now. I could speak for myself. I hesitated, but only for a moment. "I... I do."

"Come, child of winter, and sign your name upon my body."

Something was coming into view, fading in like a mirage. It was the gemstone. It floated toward me, stopping as soon as it was within arm's reach. I saw myself reflected in its shimmering blue surface, but there was something else, too. The gemstone started turning, pivoting on the spot slowly, revealing *names* etched onto its skin. There had to be hundreds of them, all beautifully carved in perfect calligraphy.

When the gemstone stopped spinning, I saw a space between the names. A moment later, I noticed a quill in my hand. There was no ink to write with, only a black quill with a metal tip. I approached the empty space, pressed the tip of the quill against the stone, and wrote my name into it as best I could.

After I had finished, the chicken scrawl I'd etched into the stone started glowing and transforming, until it settled to mimic that same perfect script all throughout.

"Henceforth, Dahlia Crowe," said the voice, "And until the end of the Royal Selection, you are an honorary guest of the city of Windhelm, and shall enjoy all the privileges and protections all of her citizens receive. May the fates shine on you."

A sharp pain pierced my hand, snapping me out of the trance *I* had fallen into. I winced, pulling my hand back and staring at my palm. A giant snowflake pattern burned bright white against my skin, but the pain was gone in an instant. A moment later, the intensity of the snowflake died down so that it looked more like a white tattoo than a glowing-hot brand.

Around me, the other competitors had experienced the same thing, only they weren't all being as… sensitive to it as I was. The girl in white, the one with the white hair, the one I had stood next to after arriving, stared at the brand on her palm with a competitive grin on her face. The girl in orange had her eyes shut and was mumbling under her breath. The other three, however, were staring directly at me.

I stared right back, switching from one to the other. They were all beautiful, all young, and all truly fae of the Winter Court. Horns, pointed ears, sharp canines, and even *wings*—they all had something about them that made them look otherworldly, strangely elegant, and incredibly deadly. I did not want to go up against them in a fight, but it was starting to look like I would have to.

Shit.

Gullie.

I ran my fingers through my hair, hoping Gullie hadn't been hit with the same magic I had. "I'm here," she whispered, once my fingers had found her, "Fae magic doesn't work so well on pixies. I doubt they know I'm even here. *Please*, don't get killed."

No promises.

A massive door opened behind the royal balcony, a sound that received a round of applause from the fae gathered around the coliseum. They'd all been so silent and still, I hadn't even noticed they were there. It was like they'd just appeared from out of nowhere, which didn't help my nerves.

I watched as the royal family emerged from behind the door, the King, Queen, and Prince taking their seats at the edge of the balcony. Around them, members of their court assembled, arranging themselves like frozen scarecrows with scowls slapped to their faces.

The King stood up from his seat, waved his hand, and said, "Let the Royal Selection… begin."

His voice echoed like thunder in a cave, followed immediately by an upbeat fanfare of trumpets, drums, and violins. Without skipping a beat, the girls arranged around the gemstone started walking toward the balcony in a single file. I fell in awkwardly at the end, following the girl in white. One by one, the girls stepped up to the space beneath the balcony, delivered a flourish and a curtsy, and then walked away from it.

I had never curtsied before in my life, it wasn't something I'd ever been taught, and watching the other girls didn't help. Witnessing their grace, their elegance, and hearing the applause each got as they had their turn in front of the royals only made me further dread my own turn. My heart was about to leap out of my chest, I feared; a feeling that only got worse once the girl in white had approached the balcony and taken her bow.

Please don't suck at this, I thought, as I prepared to move into position.

Just as I took my first few steps, the applause started dying down. The music continued, but the cheering and encouragement slowly faded until all that was left was a slight murmuring beneath the strings and the trumpets. It was like those nightmares where you turn up to an event filled with people you know only to realize after everyone's seen you that you're totally naked.

Like that, only you're not just naked, you've also got neon signs pointing at your junk.

My confident stride lost some of its power as I reached the spot where I was supposed to curtsy, nerves taking hold. I stopped, turned my eyes up at the balcony, and dared gaze at the King and Queen. Both were looking at me, but it was the Prince I noticed leaning into the edge of his seat. He was staring at me, *right* at me, waiting for me to do… something. Anything.

I could feel the heat of his gaze on my skin, the weight of it. Last night's *interaction* came rushing to the forefront of my thoughts. I found myself recalling most of it moment by moment; hearing his voice in my mind, feeling his fingers on my hand, experiencing that weird moment of connection. It was too much, too fast. I didn't know what to do.

Bow?

Curtsy?

Flip them off?

I'd already done it once, what harm could doing it a second time possibly do? *A lot, you moron.* They'd probably have me killed on the spot. At least, last time, I hadn't been pointing at the royals during my breakdown. Right now, I was directly in their sights; the entire congregation was staring at me, and I was too busy staring at their Prince.

I ripped my eyes away from him, turned to the side, and hurried to join the other girls without so much as a nod toward the royal family. That was probably going to lose me a couple of points, but it didn't sting as much as the abject silence from the fae in the stalls around the coliseum.

Already these trials had gotten off to a fantastic start.

Mira was right.

I was going to die here, but not before being utterly humiliated first.

Chapter Thirteen

I was already failing this trial. They had put me in a holding cell to await my turn, and I had no way of knowing what was happening outside. The only glimpse into the events taking place on the other side of the door were the occasional grunt, shout, and once, a low rumble of the entire room itself.

All accompanied by clapping and fanfare from the watchers.

Now that we were alone, Gullie could come out of my hair and sit on my shoulder. She was the only reason I hadn't entirely unraveled in here. I was well out of my depth, I wanted to go home, but instead I was going to be called out at any minute to take part in a physical challenge that sounded a lot like a fight.

Was I really going to be fighting something? If so, who? I didn't put it past these people to pit contestant against contestant. Knowing my luck, I would probably be made to fight the toughest, meanest contestant out there, and that would be it. I would be out. And then what?

"Do you think they'll send me back if I fail?" I asked.

Gullie frowned. "I want to say yes," she said, "But if I know anything about the fae… it's not looking good. Our best chance is to win today—or at least not lose."

"I'm glad you're here, Gull."

"Me too. Kind of."

I glanced at her, and a question popped into my head that I decided to ask. If nothing else, it would help take my mind off what was coming. "Aren't pixies and fae part of the same family?"

She shrugged. "Sort of. I mean, yes, we are. Technically. It's complicated."

"We probably have a little time?"

"Let me put this into context that I think you'll understand. You know the whole Adam and Eve myth?"

"Right…"

"Well, in one of the fae myths, Eve was told to kill Adam, but she couldn't because she loved him. She told him what she had been made to do, they defied the will of their Gods together, and were cursed for it. Both were banished from paradise, but Eve was also shrunk to my size. They loved each other, but could never be together—not in the way they wanted to—so they went their separate ways."

"So, you're technically fae."

"I am. Arcadia is my home just as much as it is theirs. But they love to treat us like we're crap anyway. I've learned not to take it personally."

"Mira said you were forbidden from entering the city…"

"The Winter Court have their own version of the creation myth in which Eve, wicked as she is, tries to kill Adam so she can eat him and gain his powers."

"That's dark…"

"I don't know if it's true or not, but they hate us all the same." She stood up on my shoulder. "Whatever happens, I'm going to be right here with you. I don't know what kind of help I can give, but I'll do my best."

I smiled at her, the nerves starting to come back. "Thanks. If we ever make it back home, I'm gonna make you so many clothes."

"You better."

The locks on the door started turning. Gullie shot back into my hair, and I got to my feet, my heart pounding. The soldier that had opened the door stared at me from behind his silver helmet, his eyes narrow, his beard thick and ginger. "Your turn," he snarled.

Swallowing hard, I took my first few steps toward destiny and the heart of the coliseum. In the distance I caught sight of the last participant being carried away. Her head was flopped over the shoulder of the soldier moving her out of the arena… and blood was dripping from her lips.

The pit in my stomach started to grow. I gripped the handle of the dagger strapped to my waist a little more tightly, but I didn't draw it. Not yet. I had to at least appear confident in front of the watchers. The fae liked a good show, remember?

"Walk to the Dais of Champions," the soldier said. "Touch the Frost Stone to begin."

I nodded and, after glancing around at the hungry crowd watching from the stands, I headed for the Frost Stone. The King and Queen were among those watching, staring at me from the far balcony. Next to them was the Prince, who like his parents, was lounging on his luxuriantly huge chair.

I had no idea what would happen the moment I touched that stone, but it was time to get this over with. No more delays. No more hesitation. No more dread. I would complete this challenge, I would pass with flying colors, and I'd make sure to keep the Prince in my sights the entire time, so he knew exactly who he was dealing with.

At least, that was the plan; whether it worked or not remained to be seen.

I pressed my fingers against the stone, and unmade the world. The ground trembled, and a gust of roaring wind enveloped me, pulling my hair in all directions. I scrambled, reaching for the dais the stone was on to try and grab it, but the platform was sinking into the ground, the blue floor swallowing the Frost Stone entirely.

I backed away from the opening in the ground as the world continued to churn and change around me. Jagged walls of ice pushed out of the ground, rapidly creating a wide circle around the spot where the stone had been. I didn't take me long to realize the walls were building a cage; a cage with me inside it.

Fingers of cold seeped from the skin of the wall at my back, a warning that I probably shouldn't touch it unless I wanted to start losing limbs to frostbite. Once the walls were up, more holes in the ground started appearing, only this time things were coming *out* of the holes. Not things, but lights; soft, blue, orb-shaped fairy lights.

The lights were scattered around the cage, but they weren't moving. Wherever they'd come out was where they stood. I watched them all for clues as to what I was supposed to do next, but found myself coming up short. Then the ground started trembling again. The hole the Frost Stone had been swallowed into opened up, and a figure emerged.

At first, I thought it was a person. A woman. But it wasn't; it was a statue. More specifically, it was an ice statue. I could see the faint white tresses of air rising from its body as the cold of the statue bled into the relative warmth around it. It was a woman, I had been right about that, but her face… it was twisted into a wide-mouthed shriek of horror, like she'd been frozen alive in an instant.

When the rumbling and the movement stopped, a voice spoke out. "Dahlia Crowe," said the same voice from yesterday—the voice without a face. "Your task is simple; collect the fairy lights scattered nearby… but beware. To attract the Hexquis' attention is to invite doom into your life."

Hexquis?

The statue?

"You have four minutes," said the voice, "Begin!"

At the sound of the gong that followed the voice, the statue burst into thousands of small shards leaving in its place a gangly looking woman with hair as black as jet, skin as white as ice, and a scream held in her lungs. The sound was horrifying. So much pain, and anguish, and anger. She threw herself on her hands and feet, clutching her eyes, and then she just kept... screaming. And screaming.

And screaming.

"Ah crap," Gullie whispered, "That's not good."

"What is it?" I said, trying not to move my lips too much.

"Dangerous. *Move*, but move quietly."

My heart broke for this woman, this creature, but the other *more rational* part of me also wanted to get nowhere near my crazy cellmate. The timer had also started ticking, so I had to move fast. With the first glowing orb firmly in my sight, I broke into a slide, gliding across the smooth, marble floor toward my destination.

I wasn't sure if I was supposed to catch the glowing light orbs or swallow them. I decided that *catch* was a safer option, so I stuck my hand out as I approached the ball of light and reached for it with my hand. The orb was warm to the touch, but it had no physical substance for me to hold onto. Instead, as soon as I touched it, the light orb shot into my forearm and burned a small, painless, circular impression into my skin.

I was about to head for the next orb, when I realized I couldn't stop sliding. I hit the wall hard with my shoulder, then fell to the floor, unable to keep my footing. Had the ground gotten slicker, somehow? I turned my eyes up to find the Hexquis staring directly at me. Her mouth hung slack and wide, and she had that same look of horror plastered on her face.

It was enough to make my heart lurch into my throat, but the worst part were her eyes. They were gone. Only black holes remained; black holes dripping with dark fluid. "I can hear you," she hissed, though her mouth never once moved.

And then she lunged toward me.

Hand over foot, she moved across the ice like her fingers and toes had spikes attached to them. My eyes widened, my entire body seizing up at the sight of the monster barreling down on me. But I had to move, I had to free myself from the paralysis and *move*, or else this thing was going to kill me.

I scrambled, but my feet could barely find any purchase on the ground. With the creature a mere few feet away from me, I grabbed my dagger, jabbed it into the wall, and used it to swing myself around just far enough that the Hexquis slammed against the section of the wall I'd been in a moment ago.

She was dazed, and scrambling herself, and still screaming.

Always screaming.

Using my dagger to get upright, I pushed myself away from the wall, and away from the Hexquis, almost without making any noise at all. As I sailed toward the next orb, I watched her thrash against the wall, gouging at it with her talon-like fingernails and desperately wishing I would never know what that felt like.

After catching the second orb, I felt like I knew what I was doing. If I moved slowly enough, I could stop myself from smashing into the wall and instead use it to move toward the next orb. The only problem was my fingers were starting to go numb. The ground had gotten so slick I'd never be able to walk on it properly. The temperature of the air had plummeted since the trial had started. And touching the wall itself was like touching frozen fire.

Nothing I could do would keep the cold at bay, and it was only getting worse.

By the time I went to catch the fourth orb, I was chattering. My heart was pounding hard, working overtime to keep my core temperature up, but I was starting to lose focus. I reached for the fourth orb—only four left to catch—but I overstretched and fell to the floor. I was so weak and numb, I hadn't been able to stop from hitting the ground with my cheek.

The sound was like a gunshot; a loud crack that filled the air.

I didn't have to see the Hexquis to know it had heard me, didn't have to look at it to know it was coming for me. What I could see, even from my low vantage, was the Prince. It was like I'd fallen in just the right place to catch sight of him standing at the edge of the balcony.

He was *standing*, not sitting. Watching intently, not with only a casual interest. To be fair, the rest of the crowd were starting to cheer, now. They'd been silent this entire time, but now that I was down, now that the Hexquis was about to swallow me whole—probably, I didn't know what she was going to do—they were elated.

It grabbed me by the foot, and that jerked a little life into me; enough that I could swing my dagger at the monster to try and get it to leave me alone. But I failed. My attack went wide. The Hexquis turned me onto my back, drove one of her clawed hands into my shoulder, and screamed into my face.

I wasn't sure what was worse, the white-hot pain of her talons ripping through my skin, or the dark hole of her mouth and what waited for me inside.

The Hexquis arched her neck back, lunged, and closed her mouth around my head.

Chapter Fourteen

Sitting upright was a mistake. An intense headrush pushed me against the pillow with the force of a much stronger pair of hands. My brain felt like a sack of loose rocks, my eyes were burning, and the ringing in my ears was relentless, but they all had nothing on the throbbing pain gripping tightly around my shoulder.

I was alive, though, and that was all that mattered. Right?

Oh no.

"Gullie!" I yelped, trying to sit up again.

"I'm here," she said, the pixie's small, glowing form looking like an indiscriminate green blob against my blurry eyesight. "I'm okay."

I sighed, relieved. "Thank the Gods. What happened?"

"Well… that thing ate your head. We had a hard time getting out of that one."

"Yeah, I thought I was going to die." I shook my head, frowning, still struggling to see. "*How* did we get out of it?"

"The Prince."

My heart gave a noticeable thump against my chest, clearing my vision up in a flash. Gullie was there, floating in front of me, her tiny fairy wings holding her aloft. She looked rough, diminished, and tired. I'd never seen that before.

"I need you to tell me everything," I said, "Because I'm worried something happened to you that you're not telling me about, but I also want to know what the Prince had to do with my trial."

"I'm fine. Trust me. I had to use more magic than usual to stay hidden, that's all. We just have to hope nobody asks you where the tattoo on the back of your neck went."

"Tat… tattoo?"

"Forget about that for now. This thing, the Hexquis, it came down on you like a clamp. I don't know how its mouth opened as wide as it did, but it swallowed your head and me up in one go. I thought we were dead. But then something hit her, hard. The next thing I know, the Prince is prying her mouth open with his hands and pulling your head out of it. I'm not gonna lie, there was blood. You were hurt. But the healers took care of it."

"Why didn't they just let it kill me?"

"That's not how they do things here. I don't know how the Royal Selection works, exactly, but I know the fae value entertainment factor above most other things. Someone dying in a trial is dramatic enough, but only for a moment. Someone suffering time after time, that's a prolonged kind of fun for them."

"That's sick."

"I know, and I'm only speaking based on what I know of them. I don't really know why they kept you alive, but that's my best guess. I'd also guess none of the other contestants are dead, either."

"Wait... so, I'm still in this trial thing?"

"You are. Mira was in here with the healers while they patched you up. She told me after they left."

"How is that possible? I failed. That thing ate me."

"Apparently today wasn't about passing or failing, but more like... figuring out who's at the front of the pack and who's at the back of the pack."

"Okay, so... do you know where I am?" Gullie's lips pressed into a thin line, then she made an *umm* sound I didn't feel too confident about. "Gull?"

"So, you're not at the top," she said, trailing off.

"Where, then? Tell me I'm somewhere around the middle of the pack. I mean, I got four orbs. That has to count for something."

Gullie winced and sucked air in through her teeth. "Yeah... no, you're not in the middle, either."

"Oh Gods... I'm at the bottom?"

"Pretty much, yeah. Bottom of the pack; way, *way* down there."

"Shit. I mean, I knew I was going to be terrible, but I thought there would at least be one or two that did worse than I did."

"No one got eaten except you, if it makes you feel any better?"

"How is that going to make me feel better?"

"Well, people never tend to forget the ones who finish first or last. So, there's that to hold onto, at least…"

I gaped at her, dumbfounded and slowly shaking my head. "I'm *last*! That can't be a good thing."

"It isn't," Mira said, exploding into the room.

"Jesus, could you *not*?" I asked, "I almost jumped out of my own skin!"

"I don't have time for pleasantries. Here, put this on."

She hurled a ball of shapeless, deep blue fabric at me that tried to wrap itself around my head. After what I'd been through, I wanted none of that, so I fought with the fabric until I managed to untangle it. Then I straightened it out and stared at it.

It wasn't shapeless, if you considered the fact that *square* was a shape. The dress was multilayered, with an unflattering neckline and back, and frills. I'd never worn something with frills in my entire life. It was hideous. Hexquis hideous.

"What… is this?"

"For you to put on."

"But it's… painful to look at. *Why*?"

"Because you were terrible out there. Just, truly, awful. And because there's going to be an event tonight, and you need to be there."

"I see you've entirely dropped your mask."

Mira shook her head. "Mask?"

"You know, the whole Custodian thing."

"Yes, well, lying to everybody else is already taxing enough on my psyche without also having to pretend around you, so I'm afraid you'll have to deal with my lack of decorum."

"I'm not complaining. I prefer knowing I'm talking to a real person rather than someone putting on an act."

"Touching, truly, but we need to get you dressed, fed, and beautified. You're already at a huge disadvantage compared to the other girls."

"What disadvantage?"

Mira sighed. "Starting with Aronia, daughter of the commander of the King's Guard, and going all the way down the list to you, each participant was given their choice of dress to pick from a luxuriant selection. They were beautiful, just stunning. The best ones were snapped up first. The one you're holding in your hand is the last one left after the carcass had been all but picked clean."

I stared at the dress on my lap. "I mean... it's not great, but by human standards, it's not terrible."

"Are you being serious? That's the most disgusting thing I've ever seen in my life. You'll be the laughing stock of the event. And trust me, they *will* laugh in your face. We're talking about the fae. You may as well drop out of the Royal Selection now."

"That's not an option. It's not like the royal family is going to put me back where they found me."

"Then, I don't know what to tell you. Tonight isn't only a meet and greet event, it's another trial."

"Trial? What are you talking about?"

Mira stepped up to me, looking desperate now. "Weren't you paying attention? I know you're human, but you must be able to process information?"

I glared at her. "I'm smart. I'm a smart person."

"You said that twice. Having to say it once is already proof enough that you're at least a little slow, so I'll explain this to you again. *Pageantry is everything here*. The fae love a show, the more glittering and glamorous it is, the better. And you can bet things will glitter twice as much out here in the frozen north because *everything* glitters. You step into that room wearing this… monstrosity, and you're finished."

"And then what happens? Because I thought I would be finished after today, but I'm still here."

"The only purpose of the trial you just went through was to set the pace for the rest of the Royal Selection. Now that the pace has been set, every other trial you go through could potentially be your last. If you fail again like you did earlier today, you could be eliminated."

I swallowed hard. "Eliminated?" I asked, "Like, killed?"

Mira frowned. "Killed? No. *Eliminated*; your trials will be over, and you'll be pulled out of the Royal Selection."

I gawked at her. "Holy shit… I really *am* in the Bachelor."

"What's the Bachelor?"

I shut my eyes. "It's a TV show back home."

"What's a… TV?"

Pinching the bridge of my nose, I sighed. "It's… really? You've never heard of a television, and *I'm* the slow one? Never mind. I can't be eliminated. If they kick me out, the question of where to send me will come up, and once that happens, everything else will follow after it. I won't be able to lie about what I am, and guess what, you go down with me."

"Me?" Mira gasped, backing away. "Why me?"

"I thought you said humans didn't pay attention. You're already in too deep. If it comes out that I'm human, at best you look like an idiot for not being able to tell, at worst you're the fae that allowed a human to exist in their city."

"A human *and* a pixie," Gullie put in.

"Right. So, you need to help make sure I don't fail tonight."

A long pause. "You might be right in your interpretation of events… but that doesn't change the fact that you will be laughed out of the trial tonight if you go in wearing that."

I looked at the dress again. A moment ago, I had thought the dress was alright, at least by human standards. But after the conversation we'd just had, the dress was starting to look more like a secondhand piece dropped in a bin at the Salvation Army. I cringed, my upper lip curling at the sight of the beast on my lap.

"I don't need to win to avoid elimination, right?" I asked. "That's how this works?"

Mira snort-laughed, a weird sound for a fae to make. "*Win?*" she asked, once she'd composed herself, "You won't win in a million years."

I frowned at her. "That's not what I asked."

"No, you don't need to win. You only need to avoid being at the bottom of the pack again."

"Do you know how they're going to grade this trial?"

"I can only guess. Aesthetics, of course, will be important; poise, choice of outfit, overall looks, that kind of thing. You'll be expected to mingle with the other contestants, and maybe even dance with the judge."

"Judge?"

"The Prince, of course."

"You mean I may have to dance with the Prince?"

Her head bobbed from side to side. "He's more likely to want to dance with those who have already caught his eye than with you… but none of this matters because you won't get through the door wearing that."

"I won't be wearing this."

She shook hear head. "You must. It's the only dress left for you, there are no others, and you must wear this dress."

"I don't need another dress, but I do need a couple of things."

"Things?"

"Is there any rule that forbids me from altering this dress?"

Mira frowned. "I, well, no. Not that I know of. But… what are you suggesting?"

"I need you to find me a needle, some thread, and maybe an enchanted sewing machine."

Chapter Fifteen

I had never worked with a sewing machine that hadn't blown up on me before. Most of the clothes I wore, I'd stitched them by hand. All of the dresses I made for other mages? Also, by hand. I couldn't tell you the amount of sewing machines I'd caused to short circuit, burn out, or simply had stopped working over the years.

It wasn't just the electric machines that didn't seem to like me, it was also the old, hand-crank ones that refused to work with me. My mothers didn't really have an explanation for it. They came to the agreement that the magic threads and fabric I would make clothes out of were simply too powerful to be put through a man-made contraption.

I accepted that idea, at least on the surface. It made sense, even if it also tripled the amount of time it took for me to fashion a made-to-order dress for another mage. I didn't have the luxury of time right now, so I needed a machine to work with. I wasn't sure if Mira would be able to get me one, or if it would even work, but we were in the land of the fae. There was magic all around.

Somewhere in this castle, I knew, there was a sewing machine I could use to turn this bland, shapeless, thing into something wearable—and I had been right.

I was lucky Mira came through.

The machine itself, like everything else about this place, was a piece of art. White, silver, and elegant; slender, but also sturdy. I had spent the better part of an hour imagining what the dress could look like and drawing up sketches; then I started cutting, passing the point of no return.

My hands had trembled the moment I slid the fabric into the machine. The needle was ready, the deep blue thread carefully woven through its many trappings and hoops. With my heart wedged in my throat I started, carefully pulling the fabric along and watching the needle move in and out, each time creating a beautiful, delicate stitch.

Gullie and Mira had both been watching the process, observing as I tried to hold it together despite the clock ticking down. There was something motivating about the threat of discovery, or death, if I messed this up, if I took too long, or if I showed up wearing a ragged, cut up monster that was even uglier than when I first got it.

Everything had to be perfect, every stitch masterful, every seam carefully and delicately woven through. But it didn't just have to be perfect, it also had to be something to marvel at, and that only made the whole project even more difficult.

The one thing I had working for me was the machine itself, and the fact that the materials I was working with were *magic*. Mira had gotten exactly the kind of materials I needed to make the dress I wanted to make.

I wanted it to dazzle anyone who looked at it, and that meant my requirements were specific; but the threads and fabric I needed were abundantly available. Not only that, I was also working with a functional sewing machine. Sure, I wished I had more time to make it with. This kind of thing would've taken me weeks to put together at home. But despite that, I was able to sew the last stitch into the dress with about an hour left before tonight's big event.

When I was done, I picked it up and held it against myself in front of the mirror. The dress was light, and soft, and elegant. The neckline plunged into my cleavage, the trail was long enough that it would follow me as I walked; I'd even had enough fabric left over to fashion a set of elbow-length gloves.

The dress had truly been enormous, and dull, and shapeless; now, hours later, I had something much, much better.

I stepped out from behind the makeshift workroom Mira had set up for me with the help of a couple of screens. Immediately Mira shot up from the couch and stared at me from across the room, her hands clasped together as if in prayer. Gullie floated into view beside the fae, leaving a trail of pixie dust in the air where she'd flown.

"Well?" Mira asked. "Can we see it now?"

"No," I said, "Not yet."

"*When?*"

"Not until I wear it."

"But... what if it's not good?"

I grinned. "There are many things I'm not good at, and I will be the first to admit it. I've been outclassed at just about everything so far, but right now, you need to trust me. I haven't seen the others, but I think even the fae will have a hard time turning their nose up at this dress."

Mira frowned. "You're asking a lot of me, there."

"Really? Not only are you aiding and abetting a human pretending to be a fae, you're also helping that human succeed in a traditional fae competition by acquiring a number of items you would prefer no one found out had gone missing. But you draw the line at trusting me?"

"I don't like the insinuation that I am in any way a criminal."

I shrugged. "I don't know what to tell you, but you're a criminal." I paused and angled my head to the side. "Can I ask you a question?"

"I have a feeling you're going to ask anyway."

"I'm British. I'm *polite*."

She rolled her eyes. "Ask your question."

"Is this the first time you've broken a rule?"

Mira's stare tightened. "No," she said, maybe a little defensively. "I've broken rules before."

I shook my head. "I mean *real* rules. The kind of rules that could get you into crazy trouble if you're found out."

"Have you?"

I nodded. "I have."

"What did you do?"

"Well… where I'm from, I make magic dresses for mages."

"Mages?"

"Yes. They're our biggest clients, in fact. Our house is filled with magic threads and fabrics acquired from all over the world. My world, and yours, actually. Materials from the land of the fae are hard to get where I live, but if you have some, you can make a lot of money for a well-made garment."

"Get to the point where you break rules."

"Right… so, even though I make magic garments for other people, I've always been strictly forbidden from making them for myself. I'm given only as much as my mothers think I need, and when I'm done, I'm asked to surrender everything I didn't use. I don't get to keep any for myself, and trust me, they use magic to make sure I'm not lying to them or hiding anything from them."

"Why are they so strict about that?"

I shrugged. "It's a number of things. The materials are expensive, and we cut costs by saving as much of it to be reused as we can. I'm also human, and flawed, and if left to my own devices, I could very well make a sweater that fills a boy with powerful feelings for me."

Mira's eyebrows rose. "What?"

"I was young. I was stupid. I was infatuated with someone who didn't feel the same way about me. So, I stole materials I wasn't supposed to use, I fashioned them into a gift, and I offered the gift to this boy for Christmas. For a time, it worked. He started liking me, so much so that he asked me to be his girlfriend. But things quickly spiraled out of control."

"This part's good," Gullie said, smiling smugly.

"You be quiet," I hissed. "Anyway, he went from boyfriend to stalker very quickly. He stopped going to school so he could wait for me around the street corner to walk me home every day. When I tried pulling away from him, he tried to hold on even tighter. Then I realized, every time I saw him, he was always wearing the sweater. Turns out, he never took it off. Two months, he wore that thing. Slept in it, too. Didn't shower in it, though. Didn't shower at all, actually. My mothers had to step in and help him."

"What happened?"

"Oh, he turned out fine. They wiped his memory of me, of the sweater, of everything bad that had happened to him since he put it on."

"Tell her what happened to you," Gullie said, her smug smile growing wider and wider.

Mira looked at her, then at me. "Yes, what did happen to you?"

Frowning, mumbling, I grumbled. "Turned me into a frog."

"A what?"

"A frog. I was a frog for a couple of days."

"That sounds… horrible."

I glanced across to the window and out toward the quiet, dark, mountainous landscape beyond the city walls. "The smell still haunts me sometimes…" I said, trailing off.

"Alright," Mira said, "I'm not someone who breaks rules."

I turned my attention to her again. "Why did you break them today?"

"Because I don't want you to lose." She paused, and for a moment, I saw something in her—something like empathy, or compassion, or even pity. Whatever it was, it was an emotion other than disdain and disinterest, and it made me happy for a time, but then the fae in her came up again. "Not because I want you to win," she added, "But because I don't want to lose."

I nodded. "Well, congratulations, Mira. You're officially a rulebreaker. We're both in this, now… to the very end."

Mira sighed. "Gods, help us."

"That was beautiful, guys," Gullie said, floating over to me. "Really. I think we just had a moment."

"Moment?" I asked.

"Look at us… a human, a pixie, and a fae, working together to trick a Prince into marriage."

"Oh, I am *not* marrying that guy. As soon as I get back to Earth, my mothers will be able to keep him from me. That's all I need."

"That's all well and good, but we need to get you there first," Mira said.

"Yes, and I'm going to need your help tonight if I'm going to get there. I don't know who anyone is, I don't know your customs, and I don't know how to act like a fae. I need you by my side. Is that going to be a problem?"

Mira frowned. "It's not… *common*, that I know of, for Custodians to accompany their wards to the first opening ball."

"Is it forbidden, though?"

"I suppose not."

"Can you get something to wear?"

She cocked an eyebrow. "I'm sure that I could. But I don't know if it is proper. There will be a lot of eyes on us if I am seen walking down the stairs with you."

"Then come with me, let them look. The more eyes on me, the better. You said the fae love pageantry, right? Well, the dress I've just made is going to knock people off their feet, but I'll need all the help I can get in… just about every other aspect of this."

Her eyes narrowed. "Is the dress truly that good?"

"It is. But I need to ask you to get me something else."

"Dahlia, no. I cannot. I have already snuck around too much. I'll get caught."

"I just need a cloak, something to wrap myself in. I don't want to reveal myself until I have the Prince in my sights."

She shook her head. "I want to help you, I do, but I can't. Not with this."

Dammit. Ever since I'd started working on the dress, I'd kept the idea of a grand reveal just for the Prince held firmly in my mind. If he casually glanced at me from across the room and was only half paying attention, there was a chance he wouldn't look at me again; a chance the dress would lose its power.

Not its magic, but its *power*.

I needed to cover it up. I needed a coat, or a cloak, or a... *"Curtain!"* I yelped, rushing over to the thick, warm, curtains falling at the sides of the long window into the great outdoors.

"Just what are you planning on doing to those curtains?" Mira asked.

"Help me get them off!" I yelled, checking for a way to pull them down.

"Are you out of your mind? You can't do that!"

"I would really love to argue this with you," I said, rushing over to my workspace and grabbing a pair of scissors, "But we already don't have enough time to get this done before the event, and wasting seconds isn't helping."

Mira watched, despairing as I tore into the curtains with my scissors, cutting whole swathes of it clean off. I tossed one at Mira, and it slapped her in the face before she could catch it. "If we get caught, don't expect me to do or say anything to defend you."

"Don't worry, I didn't think you would. Now, drop that at my workspace and go and get ready. We don't have much time."

Chapter Sixteen

The ballroom was magnificent. A wide, domed skylight gazed up into the starlit heavens. Below it, crowds of Courtiers gathered to talk, and mingle, and drink from long-necked glasses being served by young males and females in finely cut suits.

Soft music flowed as I approached the set of grand stairs that would take me down into the thick of things. From the top, I got a good glimpse at all the many blues and whites and silvers of the luxurious space I was about to set foot in.

I'd never been anywhere nearly as fancy before. I just wasn't the type to go to lavish parties where everyone gets dolled up to eat, and drink with other, equally well-groomed people. I much preferred my own company, thank you very much. All that was to say nothing about the crippling social anxiety I'd had to fight my entire adolescence.

A room full of people pressed closely together was literally one of my nightmares, and I was about to step into one willingly today.

"Back straight," Mira hissed, "Chin up, and walk with grace. Is this the first time you've worn a pair of high heels?"

"No," I snapped, following Mira's instructions, "This is the *third* time I've worn high heels."

"You look like you're walking on stilts. Let your instincts guide you."

"My instincts are telling me to turn tail and get out of this place before it eats me alive. Should I do that?"

"Absolutely not. You are to dive into that ballroom and dazzle the world with your creation, or so help me."

"So help you, *what,* exactly?"

"I'm… not sure, but I would find some way of exacting vengeance on you for abandoning your duties here."

"Will you guys stop arguing?" Gullie hissed, "People are already watching".

She was hiding in my hair, again. Mira had insisted that letting my hair fall lazily over my shoulders didn't quite fit the look the way an updo would have. She was certain it would cost us points not to show off my slender neck. But I needed Gullie to be where she was, otherwise this was all over, so my silver hair remained long and wavy.

"Sorry," I said, "I'm just nervous."

"I get that," Gullie said, "But you have to impress the Prince and his parents if you want to earn his trust."

I shook my head. "I hate this. I hate him for stealing me from my home, I don't want to be anywhere near him."

"But you have to be. I know you can do this, and you know it too. Now, go and be the incredible person you are."

I smiled at myself as I reached the top of the stairs. "Thanks, Gull," I said, scanning the room from above. The King and Queen were present, sitting at a table on a raised dais, overseeing the party as it unfolded beneath them. I couldn't help but notice the empty seat at the King's left hand. That meant the Prince was in the mix, somewhere.

"I don't see him," I said.

Mira took my chin in her fingers and turned my head slightly. "There," she said.

And there he was, decked out in all his finery, wearing a fitted black suit that stood in stark contrast against all the blues and whites around him. He looked incredible. Flawless. Regal. I didn't know how I'd missed him, although he *was* being beset by about five other women, so that was probably it.

"Shit," I said. "He isn't even going to notice me."

"Then we'll have to just get their attention," Mira said, grinning and turning her palm upward. In her hand, a whole cluster of little stars were being born. With a quick flick of her wrist, she sent them shooting through the air where they burst into thousands of much smaller motes of light that fell across the ballroom like rain.

Everyone's eyes turned to us, my nightmare now coming fully to life. I couldn't hesitate, I couldn't flinch away from this. I pressed my fingers against the clasp of the cloak I had quickly fashioned out of a set of curtains and tore it off with one quick move. Then the gown underneath came to life, the magic inside flaring out from within.

The dress itself was the deep blue of a starless night, but with a touch of magic, a glittering starfield erupted across it. Some of those stars burned brighter than others, and between them, links of silvery light started to form full constellations that moved and shifted along the gown. It didn't just sparkle and change with the light; looking at the dress was like looking into the heavens themselves.

Mira had turned heads, and now I was keeping their attention. Doing my best not to lose what little grace I had, I started slowly descending the stairs, making my way into the press of Courtiers and contestants.

I noticed Mareen, Kali, and Verrona glaring at me from where they stood. They all looked impeccable, and their dresses were gorgeous. Mira told me they had each placed quite high during the first trial—top six, in fact, with Aronia standing as the current frontrunner. I didn't know what she looked like, but Mira was able to point her out as one of the women I'd noticed yesterday.

The only woman who had dared to be seen eating.

She wasn't eating now, but she also wasn't standing anywhere near the Prince. Her dress was the most beautiful of them all; black as pitch, deeply cut at the chest and back, and hugely flattering not only to her feminine physique, but also emphasizing her strong, physical qualities. Like the others, she was looking at me from where she stood; unlike the others, I didn't think she gave a crap about my dress, her dress, or anyone else's.

I already liked her.

"Now," Mira said, standing close to me as we reached the bottom, "Be calm and composed, and *keep your bloody chin up.*"

"Should I go to the Prince right away?"

"Heavens, no. Wait for him to come to you. Be alluring, play hard to get. But remember, it isn't just the Prince you want to impress—you're also trying to impress his parents."

By the time we reached the bottom, the conversation, and the music, seemed to rise back to normal levels. Some rogue eyes never left the back of my head, but most of the fae in the ballroom seemed more interested in themselves and what they were doing than in me. Right at this point, I was happy for their narcissism.

A servant whisked past us with a plate in his hand. Mira plucked two of the long-necked glasses on the plate and handed one over to me. It was filled with the same blue liquid the Prince had tried to make me drink last night.

"Okay, this blue stuff is everywhere," I said, "What is it?"

Mira had already taken a sip. "This? It's *Clair di Lune*. Drink, it's really nice."

I stared at the drink, still unsure. "The Prince tried to give me some."

"It's wine made from berries that only grow here, and only when the earth and the air are at their coldest—so, around now."

Frowning, I brought the glass to my lips and tipped it back. The liquid was ice cold, but so sweet, so rich, I couldn't help but drink and swallow. Cold, and smooth, it slid down my throat sending a chill racing through my entire body. I thought I hated it, but then it started reminding me of the pie I'd eaten last night, so I went in for another sip.

"Verdict?" Mira asked.

I visibly shuddered, then licked my lips. "It's kind of delicious."

"Isn't it just?"

"Alright," I scanned the ballroom again, then subtly gestured at Aronia. "What can you tell me about her? She's the one at the top right now, correct?"

"First thing you need to know about her, she's amazing. Her father is the Commander of the King's Guard and has been for four decades, which means she's lived in a military family her entire life."

"Forty years is a long time."

"Not in fae years, but it's also not insignificant. From the moment she was born, everyone knew she would one day take the Prince's hand, and so far, she's proving everyone right."

"She looks incredible in that dress… and those muscles. *Crap*. I don't stand a chance against her."

"No. You don't."

"That's really encouraging."

"I'm here to advise you and to tell you the truth. Unless she is somehow knocked out of the Royal Selection, she will probably win."

"So… what do we do?"

"We focus on beating the ones you can beat. We focus on keeping you in this competition for as long as possible."

I gestured with a nod over to Mareen. "Her," I said, "I want to beat her."

Mira laughed so hard she almost spat some of her wine. "Could we please pick targets we know we can beat?"

"Even in a world where most of the people are jerks, she's the worst jerk of them all. She needs to go down a peg or two."

"I don't think you understand. There's an elimination process involved, here, but elimination isn't only dependent on passing or failing trials. You can fail a trial and stay in the race, or you can pass a trial but still be eliminated."

"How does it work, then?"

"Usually, and this is my first Royal Selection, so I don't know if things have changed, when it comes time to eliminate someone, it always boils down to a big trial in which all contestants are pitted against each other in a challenge to determine who is eliminated. Those who have done well in previous trials are given an advantage. Those who do badly, are penalized. Most of the time it's only one that goes, but as far as I know, there's no rule stopping the royals from eliminating more than one at a time."

I shook my head, and the world tipped a little bit. "Holy hell," I said, blinking hard. "Is that the wine already?"

Mira laughed. "I should have warned you, it's strong, especially to those who haven't quite built up a tolerance yet."

I set the glass down at the next available plate, half finished. That was all it had taken. "Good thing I refused the Prince," I said, breathing deeply to fight off the wine's effects.

"I think it would've been hilarious if you had passed out in front of the Prince, but that's just me."

I scowled at her. "*Moving swiftly on*. You still haven't told me why I can't just go and make myself look better than Mareen. Wouldn't that kind of thing keep me out of the bottom three on its own?"

"Something about this place I don't think you've quite grasped yet, is the matter of *status*. It's important to the fae. If you're ranked at the bottom, the royals are going to expect you to interact, and fight with, those of your status. If you, the lowest ranked contestant, suddenly walked up to Mareen and tried to make her look bad, you'd be instantly ridiculed. It would lose you even more points."

"Did you just basically tell me to stay in my lane?"

"I… don't understand. Lane?"

"It's something we say on Earth." I sighed. "So, what you're saying is I need to find the other girls near my status and make sure I'm better than them."

"Ideally, yes."

"And how do I improve my status?"

"By passing your trials with style and not getting eaten. The only thing to consider right now is this; under no circumstances should you do anything that makes you look like you're reaching above your station. That could be… just, catastrophic for your chances."

I nodded. "Alright, I think I get it. I'll just stay in my lane. I can do that. I can—"

Mira sucked in a harsh breath, her eyes widening. I felt a finger tap against my shoulder, and when I turned, there he was… Prince Cillian himself, in the flesh. My insides froze quicker than when they'd been hit by that ice-cold wine. On the plus side, I sobered up in a flash.

He was hot, so damn hot. His hair was brushed back and pulled into a bun behind his head, his white horns running along the curve of his skull. I noticed now, maybe for the first time, that while his ears did end in points, they weren't as pointed as the other fae in the room. He also had sharper canines than most, canines that flashed when he smiled.

Like now.

I hated that he was so damn attractive. I hated that I couldn't say I wasn't drawn to him. But he was also the reason I was here; and I hated him for that, most of all.

"My Prince," Mira said, with a little curtsy.

I mirrored her movements. "My Prince," I added.

He stared at me, his cold, blue eyes sharp and piercing. "Come with me," he said, extending his hand. "You'll dance with me."

It wasn't a request, or a question; it was a demand. One I couldn't ignore, one I couldn't slap aside. I was starting to get the hang of this place, and even I knew to deny the Prince's order to dance with him would lose me a ton of points, if it didn't get me kicked out of the competition outright.

I took his hand and followed him deeper into the room, where the music started to swell even if I couldn't hear it over the sound of my own heart. I glanced over at Mira as I walked away, shock and terror written on my face.

"Be graceful," she said, moving only her lips.

Be graceful… with the Prince. Sure, easy, no problem. I'm screwed.

Chapter Seventeen

The feel of his hand on my lower back made my skin tingle. It wasn't only that he was big, the firmness of his touch, or the heat radiating from his muscular body. It also wasn't the beard, or the hair, the horns, or even his sharpened canines that triggered my body's most primal instincts.

It was the way he *smelled*.

I hadn't been this close to a man in years, not since my last relationship fell through. I had mostly forgotten about him in the time that had passed. The way he spoke, the way he laughed, the way his voice pitched up whenever we'd argue. But there was one thing I hadn't forgotten, and that was his scent.

It had been a warm, homely scent that made me think of fireplaces, burned wood, and… old socks. I couldn't say when the first time I'd detected that final scent had been, but it became difficult to live with as the months rolled on.

It wasn't that he personally had bad hygiene, he didn't. I just couldn't escape the aroma whenever I was near him, and even now, long after we parted ways, I couldn't light a fireplace, or handle an old sock, without thinking about him, even if just for a moment.

The last man I had gotten close to had exuded an aroma of mediocrity, of *meh*. Cozy, warm, but *meh*. Prince Cillian, on the other hand? His scent bowled over me like a wave. It wasn't warm, it was *scalding hot*, as if inside him burned a cold star whose heat only those that dared get this close to him could feel.

It was perfumed, but masculine—I felt safe, and also like I was in grave danger. At the same time, it conjured images of the furry blanket you wrap yourself in when the temperature plummets, and the bristly fur on the back of a snarling wolf as it stalks you through the snow.

I kept my eyes glued to his muscular chest as my internal systems went into overdrive. I feared that looking into his eyes would send me running in the other direction, and yet part of me didn't want to let my hands fall from his shoulders as we swayed and meandered through the ballroom. It was as if I could feel his skin vibrating beneath my fingertips, through his clothes.

I didn't know what to do, so I let myself be silently led in a slow waltz while my heart decided whether to leap out of my throat or calm the hell down.

Mira, frantically, tried to make eye contact with me. I could see her zipping through the crowd, bobbing in and out of view as I moved with the Prince. She was trying to keep me from doing or saying something stupid, but I had a feeling even her best efforts were doomed to fail here.

"Your dress," the Prince said, trailing off.

I couldn't see his eyes. I didn't dare. "Yes?" I asked, keeping my voice low.

"It's not what I expected to see you wearing."

"You expected to see me?"

A pause. "You and all the others. Who gave you that dress?"

"This is the dress I was given."

"That is a gown fit for a Princess. Are you a Princess?"

"I am not." I turned my eyes up only to find him looking directly down at me. I swallowed hard. "I made it myself."

His eyebrows arched. "You made it?"

"I'm a seamstress, but I suppose you didn't know that."

"I did not. That is why I'm here."

I narrowed my eyes at him. "Is it? Aren't there other girls you should be dancing with? Like her?" I nodded over at Aronia.

"She will have her moment. But you intrigue me."

"Why?"

The Prince twirled us both, making the room spin. I was glad his presence had sobered me up, otherwise I didn't think I would've recovered from the movement as quickly as I did. When the world returned to normal, our last interaction came to mind. I'd basically fled from his room, and now we were here, dancing and chatting as if that hadn't happened.

"I watched your trial," he said.

"I think it was a little hard to miss."

"True. You put on quite the show."

"I got eaten. Does that count?"

"It does. Even though you clearly lack experience and training, you know how to entertain. That will get you far."

He thinks it was intentional. I wanted to laugh, but I couldn't. "Yes, well, that's what we're here for, isn't it? I didn't do it on purpose—I wanted to win so I wouldn't get eliminated."

"You didn't mean to treat the crowd as well?"

"Not really. I hate attention."

His eyes narrowed, then dipped below my neck line, making my skin flush red where his eyes roamed. "And yet, your dress… how could you have created something so impressive in such little time?"

"I told you. I'm a seamstress—I'm good at making dresses."

"Perhaps, but you did not need create anything even half as dazzling as this to merely stave off elimination. This dress tells me you wish to be seen, or part of you does, anyway."

"Does it?"

"I see you, *Dahlia*… the question is, what would you do with my attention?"

That's one hell of a question.

The simple answer was, I wanted him to send me home. The truth was starting to feel a lot more complicated than that. Because the truth was, he was right. There was something between us. I could feel it in my gut. It was something like familiarity, like knowing, but I didn't know him. I had never met him before recently, I had never been to this world, I wasn't *from* this world.

But there was, undeniably, something there… and whatever it was, it was getting stronger; coming closer to the surface.

"I don't want anything from you," I said.

The Prince's upper lip curled and he pulled me a little closer to his body. *"Liar,"* he growled, his voice sending shivers up my spine. "Everybody wants something from me."

I took a second to compose myself. "I want to do well in the trials."

"You and everyone else, but I fear none of you truly understands what waits for you at the end of this process."

"We were all told. I'm sure we're prepared."

"I'm not sure that you are, Dahlia. I'm not sure anyone is ready for what's coming."

I frowned at him. "Coming?"

The Prince twirled me again, spinning me around and pulling me back to him. "Do you believe in fate?"

"Fate? What do you mean?"

"Do you believe destiny plays a role in our lives? That there are things about our lives that were predetermined, possibly before we were even born?"

"I… I don't think I know what you mean."

He wrapped one hand around the small of my back and pressing my chest against his. I felt my chin tip upwards, my lips loosen. I could feel his breath against my face, cool and warm at the same time. "I think you do," he whispered.

My heart thundered. We were so close together, I thought he'd be able to feel it, or maybe even hear it. That was the last thing I wanted, for him to know how excited I was, how fearful I was, how *turned on* I was.

I tried to pull away, but the Prince was a lot stronger than me and he held me in place.

"Let me go," I said.

"I need to know," he said.

"Know what?"

"I need to know… *why you*."

Why me. The words reverberated inside of me like I was hollow. I stared at him, watching his lips, *fixed* on his lips. They were so close, an inch or two of movement and we'd kiss. I despised myself for wanting to know what it would feel like to kiss him, to fly so close to the star burning inside of him. But I also knew doing so was dangerous. I didn't know him, I didn't trust him, and everything about him screamed *lethality*.

"My Prince," came a soft, sweet voice from off to the side.

His grip on me loosened the moment his attention was divided. I took the chance to slip out of his grasp and pulled away. Mareen was there, resplendent in a golden gown that looked like it was made of light itself. She curtsied before him, smiling.

"May I perhaps have the privilege of a dance with his Highness?" she asked, returning to standing.

The Prince looked at her for a long, hard moment, then back at me. As soon as his attention was turned away from her, Mareen scowled. Glaring, she made her intent clear to me. Get between her and the Prince, and she was going to pull my hair clean off my scalp. That, however, I wasn't nearly as worried about as I was at the thought of spending another moment next to *him*.

Swiftly, I curtsied, and made a rapid escape back into the press of Courtiers and contestants. I didn't stop to look for Mira, I didn't make eye-contact with anyone else. To hell with this trial, to hell with getting points.

I couldn't stand the thought of being in that room for another moment. My heart was pounding, my hands were trembling, and my chest had tightened to the point where I thought my ribs would implode. I was, well and truly, in the jaws of a panic attack. My *flight* instinct had been triggered, but I managed to stop myself from fleeing like I had from the Prince's room the other night. Instead, my exit was elegant and tempered.

It was only when I found a dark corner to slide into where I let the mask break.

Gullie zipped out of my hair and floated in front of me. I wanted to hiss at her to get back inside, to avoid being seen, but I couldn't speak; I could barely breathe. Without hesitating, Gullie blew a cloud of fairy dust into my face and started whispering comforting words against my ear. It wasn't until Mira found us that I'd managed to gather enough of myself to speak.

"Dahlia," she said, throwing her arms up. "What are you doing here?" Mira batted the air in front of her nose, suddenly recoiling. "It smells like harpy around here," she hissed.

"Pixie," Gullie hissed.

"What happened?" Mira asked.

"What did it look like?" I asked.

"It looks like you decided to leave only moments after arriving."

"It didn't look like I was crazy?"

Mira shrugged. "A little eccentric, maybe, but I wouldn't say you looked crazy. *What happened*?"

I shook my head. "The Prince. He's… intense."

"He is known for that, yes. Even outside of the Winter Court, Prince Cillian has a reputation."

"I don't know how to deal with it."

"My dear, you're going to learn, sooner or later. Winning the Royal Selection comes with—"

"Marriage? Trust me, I don't intend on that ever happening." Mira approached, frowning and stretching a concerned hand my way. I didn't take it. "He talked about fate," I said, still trying to piece myself together.

"What did he say?"

"He thinks he knows me… thinks I'm someone I'm not."

"Who does he think you are?"

"I don't know," I snapped, "Someone important enough that he picked me up tonight to dance with instead of dancing with those other, higher up girls. He made me look like an idiot, and then he asked *why you*, like he was repulsed."

Mira came a little closer and *took* my hand. "I don't understand."

"Neither do I. Why me, *what*?"

After a moment of pause, of silence, possibly of hard thinking, she wrapped an arm around my shoulder and brought me out of the nook I had been hiding in. "We need to get you upstairs," she said.

"But what about the trial?"

"Forget about that for now. I need you to tell me everything he said."

Chapter Eighteen

Mira rushed into my room with a bottle of *Claire de Lune* in her hand. With a click of her fingers, the bottle's cork popped, then she handed the bottle over to me. I was sitting on the floor, my gorgeous, constellation dress a puddle around my body.

"Drink," she said, "It'll calm your nerves."

She didn't have to ask me twice. The wine was likely to knock me out quick, but I grabbed the bottle by the neck and I took a swig. Though the bottle and the wine were cold, the drink eventually started to warm my body from the inside out. Shuddering from the sudden and sharp changes in internal temperature, I took another drink.

"I screwed it up," I said, staring at the floor. I drank again, and deep. I didn't stop until Mira yanked the bottle out of my hand. "Hey, I wasn't done."

She pressed the bottle to her lips. "Save some for me," she said, and then she took a long drink before setting the bottle down.

Gullie fluttered out of my hair and settled on the back of the dining chair nearby. "Any chance there's a pixie-sized cup somewhere for me to drink from? I want to get buzzed, too."

"I shouldn't care," Mira said, "But I worry drinking Claire de Lune would kill you, little harpy."

"Pixie, and you're not my mother."

Mira laughed, then drank. "Good one."

She handed the bottle over to me, and I knocked back another swig. "Trust me, Gull. You'll hate this."

"Then why are you drinking it?" she asked.

"I… can't seem to stop."

Mira took a deep sigh, then exhaled. "Well, *that*… could've gone better," she said.

"You think?"

"It could also have gone far, far worse. Needless to say, we made an impression tonight."

"Maybe, but I vanished from the party barely twenty minutes after getting there. That couldn't have been good."

"It was an unmitigated disaster, yes, but it could still have been worse."

"How?"

"Well, you looked great. Better than most of the other women there. That counted for something." She clicked her fingers, like she'd just been inspired. "Oh! Mysterious! That's it, you probably created an air of mystery about you. That's what we'll say if someone asks."

Already the room had started to spin a little. I blinked hard and looked up at Mira to try and stabilize myself. "If who asks?"

"I don't know. Anyone. The less people see you and know about you, the more they'll want to know. It'll intrigue them. That's how we'll keep you in the competition."

"But I don't want people to… want to know me."

"That's just it, they never will. We'll make sure of that." Mira grabbed the bottle again and took a drink before extending it to me.

I took the bottle and cocked my head. "I just realized something."

"What?"

"You're getting drunk with a human."

She rolled her eyes. "Don't remind me. Just drink."

"Won't I need to be sharp for tomorrow's trial?"

"There won't be a trial tomorrow. Tomorrow, you'll have the run of the castle. Though, ideally, you'll use the day to train as much as you can to prepare for the next trial. You know, considering how far behind you are."

I frowned, then drank. "That sounds like loads of fun."

"It's not meant to be fun. Anyway, I want you to tell me what happened with the Prince. He is the reason why you're here, and if he's interested in you, we need to try to capitalize on that."

"You saw most of what happened, didn't you?"

"I saw him whisk you away to dance. You can't dance, by the way. Has anyone ever told you that?"

I stared at her, bemused. "You're the first."

She extended her hand, expecting the bottle. I handed it back, and she drank, but she never sat down. "So, he took you to dance, then what?"

"We spoke, he asked a lot of questions, I tried to avoid them." I shook my head, but that only made the world tilt and start jiggling. No amount of blinking settled it. I felt myself about to topple over, so I stuck my hands out and planted them against the floor.

Mira made a frustrated moan. "You *humans* can't handle your wine."

"Sorry… I'm a lightweight even by human standards."

Mira wrapped her hands under my arms and hoisted me up. My fae mentor was stronger than she looked, and with her help, I made my way over to the bed and sat down. I held myself upright for a moment, but gravity got the better of me, and I fell into the plush pillows like a rock.

"*Belore*," I sighed, letting my eyes close *just for a moment*.

A pause.

"What did you just say?" Mira asked.

I opened my eyes again. "What?"

"Either you're already talking nonsense, or you just spoke royal fae."

Laughing, I let my eyes close again. "Psht. I don't know *fae*, how am I going to know royal fae?"

"You tell me."

I heard the word again in my mind, and my eyes shot open. I stared at Mira, though for a moment I thought there were two of her. My heart started pounding, adrenaline quickly flooding through my system and helping me rise above the drunken pit I was falling into.

The seconds were ticking over, and I was just staring at her. Blankly. I realized, then, I hadn't quite told her everything yet. For instance, she had no idea that I'd already met the Prince once before coming here, in the human world.

She didn't know he had picked me up from the street, or that he'd grabbed my shoulders and plunged his nose into my hair. I hadn't told her that he'd used that word the moment we'd met. That it had been the first thing he'd ever said to me. I wasn't sure why I hadn't told her until now, , but I didn't think I could keep it to myself any longer.

Especially if the Claire de Lune had anything to do with it.

"I… it's something the Prince said to me," I said.

Mira's eyebrows both went up. "The Prince," she said, "He said *that* word, specifically. You're sure you didn't hear it wrong?"

"If I had heard it wrong, I would've said it wrong, and we wouldn't be having this conversation."

She paused, considering this. "True... if you'd failed to correctly enunciate the word, I would be laughing at you for butchering our beautiful language."

"See? I must be telling the truth."

Mira straightened up, walked over to the table where she'd left the bottle, and shooed Gullie off the rim.

"Hey, I was trying to drink that," Gullie yelled.

"Trust me, little harpy. This drink will incapacitate her, and it will kill you." With a curt, frustrated smile, she pressed the bottle to her lips, and *finished* it. There must've been more than half a bottle left, yet when she set it back down on the table, it was empty.

A tense moment passed where Mira seemed a little off balance. She reached for the table, but missed, caught the neck of the bottle, and it fell onto its side—but it didn't smash. An instant later, she corrected herself and stood upright. She then picked up a napkin from the table and gently dabbed the corners of her mouth.

Finally, she shuddered like a tree trying to shake off a week's worth of snow. "*Much* better," she said.

I gaped at her. "What... the hell? Why aren't you drunk?"

She ran a hand through her hair, fixing it up. "My older brother owns one of the vineyards. I grew up drinking this."

"They let kids drink alcohol here?"

"Hush now, *human woman*." She took a circle of the room before stopping and looking at me. "It's possible he's gone insane."

"He's what?"

"Insane. Mad. You see, there's absolutely no reason whatsoever why he would've said that to you. To someone else, sure. I could believe it. But to you? A peasant from the human world?"

"*Hey*, that stings."

"*I said hush*," she hissed. "The word itself is old; very old. It is from a time when our people were far more superstitious than we are now, more tribal, less refined. When we vehemently believed in the fates, and in destiny."

"The Prince talked about all that…"

"Yes, his superstitious behaviors don't go unnoticed. Rumor has it he plucks exactly six white roses from his personal garden and has them woven into his cloak before he goes into battle."

"That's… strange, but not, I mean, it's not insane behavior."

Mira stared at me. "If those same white roses don't come back red with blood, he spills the blood of a servant upon them."

"Oh." My stomach churned. "Okay, that is pretty psychotic."

"Do you see? He *must* be insane. Why else would he have named you his *belore*? It doesn't make sense. That happens at the *end* of the selection."

"Oh my God, could you tell me what the word means already?"

Mira lowered her eyes. "Where's your sense of theatre, *human*? I'm getting to it, but you need context first. See, there's a reason for the royal selection beyond simple vanity or entertainment. There's also a reason why the winner of the selection is set to marry the Prince."

"Because you guys live in a patriarchy where young women have no better prospects than to marry rich?"

A frown darkened the fae's face. "That isn't funny."

"I thought it was funny."

"*Anyway, o*nce the contest is over, fate itself manifests to join the royal and the winner as each other's *belore*." She paused. "You would say *soulmate*."

Soulmate.

The word rang out inside of me, making my skin prickle and my chest flush with warmth. "No, that can't be right."

"It is. It has happened many, many times."

"But I haven't won the selection." I shook my head. "And... he said it before I even knew I was in it. Before I'd even come here."

Mira's head cocked to the side. "What do you mean?"

"In the human world. I saw him, before I was kidnapped and brought here. He sniffed me, and then he called me his... soulmate. And you know what? Now the whole *why you* question makes sense. He thinks I'm his soulmate, and he doesn't know why."

"He can't possibly think you're his soulmate. The selection decides, not the Prince."

"How can the selection decide? It's just a stupid competition."

"I told you. *Fate.* Haven't you been paying attention?" She stuck her hand out. "Don't answer that. Of course, you haven't. And I can't expect your human mind to possibly understand the nuances of the kind of ancient, fae magic that surrounds this entire process."

"See, here's the thing. Whoever he thinks I am, *I'm not her*. Someone made a mistake when they targeted me to be brought here."

Mira stared at me, tapping her foot, her arms folded in front of her chest. "Well, *obviously*. You're as socially adept as a wax candle, you can't fight, you don't know magic, and you're not even fae."

"Which *means*, whoever I'm supposed to be is still out there, somewhere. Or maybe something happened to her and she needs help. Doesn't that worry you?" I stuck my hand out this time. "Actually, no, don't answer that. I know it doesn't. How are fae chosen to participate in the selection?"

"I… I don't know the answer to that. I assume it comes down to station, or breeding… all I know is, the selection itself is sacred. The contestant must be brought to the great hall at high noon on the coldest day of the year, and then made to participate."

"We need to figure that out, because I'm not supposed to be here, I'm not supposed to be in this stupid competition, and I'm *definitely* not Prince Cillian's soulmate."

"Yes…" she trailed off, "Yes, on all those things, we are in agreement." Mira paused. "Get some sleep. Tomorrow, rest, eat, and train. You are also allowed to visit the library—if you're going to be staying here a while, it would be good for you to read a little of our history. Your harpy can help."

Silence. I'd expected to hear Gullie's protest, but it didn't come. Looking at the table across the room, I found the pixie lying on her back, under the toppled bottle of Claire de Lune with her mouth open, lapping up droplets as they fell. Frowning, Mira grabbed the bottle and picked it up.

"I thought I told you not to drink this," she said.

"I'm not known for taking advice," Gullie said, followed by a hiccup. She brought her head up to look at me, cocked a thumbs up, and then passed out.

I followed soon after, putting a close to one hell of a long day.

Chapter Nineteen

I dreamt of home that night, and woke up in tears the next morning. I missed my house, my room, my mothers. I missed my cups of tea and hot chocolate, mother Pepper's hot scones, mother Evie doing my hair to make sure I take care of it, mother Helen's authoritarian brand of care and affection.

I wanted so badly to be back home, it almost felt like a physical weight sitting on my chest. I didn't want to get out of bed. I didn't want to eat breakfast. But I forced myself up. I had to. There was no way I could spend the day in bed, not when my next trial was tomorrow.

Not when my home was waiting for me to come back.

After picking at some of the food that had been left for me in the morning, I headed out of my room to find a tall man clad in full-plate armor standing by my door. I saw my own reflection in his chest-plate, and thanked my stars that my glamor had held overnight because I hadn't bothered to check before leaving the room.

The man who was easily three times my size looked down at me. He was wearing a helmet, so all I could see were his chin, his thick orange beard, and his clear blue eyes. "Yes?" he asked in a deep, gruff voice.

"Uh, hello," I said, "I would like to go to the library."

Silence from the guard.

"Please?"

His eyes narrowed. "This way," he grunted, and then he started down the stairs that led away from my room. I followed, silently falling into step behind him as he led me through the castle. I felt a little strange being babysat by a mountain of a man, but I was grateful to have him around once I noticed the eyes that were following me.

Everywhere I went, winter courtiers in mid-conversation would stop and stare at me. Some would whisper, murmur to each other. Some would eye me up and down from afar, as if they were trying to size me up.

Hiding behind the mountain all the way to the library, I avoided making eye contact with anyone. Just in case they got the wrong idea and decided to come up and talk to me. As soon as I reached the large set of double doors that led to the library, the guard stood aside, grabbed the handle, and pulled them apart for me to walk through.

My mouth fell as I stepped inside. The castle library was magnificent, brightly lit, and encased in another domed, glass ceiling into which the gorgeous winter sun freely shone. I stared up into the clear, winter sky, shielding my eyes from the sun's brightness with my hand.

Directly beneath the dome were a number of ornate, wooden tables and chairs where people could comfortably read, but the library itself was dead quiet. I was the only person here. Well, me, Gullie, and the guard—but the guard didn't follow us into the library. Instead, he waited near the door, watching disinterestedly from a distance.

I didn't have any instructions as to what the rules here were, so I decided to head into the nearest set of stacks and start exploring. The aisles were long, and deep; rows, upon rows, upon rows all filled to the brim with books, not a single one of them dusty or worn out. I, alone, didn't have a hope in hell at finding what I wanted. Not because the place was huge, but because I couldn't read a word of fae.

Lucky for me, I had a *Gullie* to help.

"Why is it the fae speak English?" I asked.

"They aren't speaking English," Gullie said.

I was sitting in the stacks, cross-legged, with a book in my lap and several others scattered around me. Gullie went from page to page, carefully tiptoeing across them and reading aloud when she heard something interesting.

"They aren't?" I asked, "Then how do I understand them?"

"It's magic. The fae love the sound of their own voices, the last thing they want is for someone to not understand their perfectly crafted sentences and impeccable decorum."

"Mira is lacking in that department a little bit. I watched her chug nearly a whole bottle of wine last night."

"Yeah, she's… a weird one. In her defense, we did sucker punch her with the whole *you're a human* thing."

Gullie stopped on a page and carefully studied a passage of tightly woven scribbles. It was supposed to be written in *ancient fae*; difficult to read even by normal standards. That Gullie could read it at all, and as quickly as she was reading, was impressive.

"What's up?" I asked.

"Okay…" she said, trailing off, "So, Windhelm is about eleven *thousand* years old."

"Didn't Mira say it had stood for ten thousand years?"

"Yeah, those first thousand years were a little rocky. Anyway, according to this, that Frost Stone you wrote your name into, it was found buried in the snow by a group of explorers who first ventured this far north. After it was excavated, the fae who found it decided to build a settlement around it. That settlement eventually became this city."

"Wow… we have old cities back on Earth, but that's crazy."

"There have been fourteen Kings and seven Queens, eight Royal Selections, six attempted invasions by enemies of the Winter Court, and two magical… incursions? I think I'm reading that right."

"What's an incursion?"

"I'm not sure. It sounds dark, though. I mean, a war is a war, fae fighting fae. In an incursion, it sounds like it's the fae fighting… something else."

"Do you know what that something else is?"

"No. It doesn't say. The last incursion was… over two hundred years ago. The one before that happened around another two… *thousand* years earlier."

Gullie skipped over a couple of pages until we came upon some family trees. It wasn't long until we found the Wolfsbane tree. *The Prince's family*. Gullie walked along the tree, repeating names as she read them until, finally, she stopped at the tippy top of the tree. Written there, were four names.

Yidgam Wolfsbane and Haera Wolfsbane.

The King and Queen.

Branching away from them, however, were another two names. Cillian Wolfsbane… and *Radulf* Wolfsbane.

"Holy crap," I said, the Prince has a brother?

"*Had*," Gullie said. "See this? His name has been crossed out. That means he's dead."

"Dead… the Prince has a dead brother."

"I'm not sure if that's something he wants us knowing."

"It's in a history book, though, right? That means this is public knowledge."

"Yeah, but Radulf's name hasn't just been crossed out. Look."

Other deceased members of the family tree had their names delicately crossed out, with crescent moon symbols hanging above them. With Radulf, it looked like someone had taken the business end of a quill and scratched it through a bunch of times. It was almost illegible, and his name didn't have a crescent moon hanging off it.

"What do you think that means?" I asked.

"I don't know," Gullie said. "We should probably ask Mira about it. If anyone will be able and willing to tell us, it's probably going to be her."

"I'm not sure we should," I said, picking the book up and closing it. "The less I know about this family, the better."

"Are you really telling me you don't want to know more about this place and its people? You don't want to read more about *belore?*"

"*Gods*, no. I want nothing to do with that. And as for the rest, we've been reading for a little while, and so far we've learned this city is old, it's got a bloody history, there's probably monsters in the north, and the Prince had a brother who I haven't heard mentioned once since I've been here. It's all been bad."

"That bit about the Frost Stone was good," Gullie said, a little meekly.

"Yes, that was good. The stone is interesting, but it probably also has a dark past we don't know about yet. Coming here was a mistake."

I went to stand, when I heard footsteps moving closer to the mouth of the aisle I was in. Gullie shrieked *shit* and darted into my hair. I grabbed the book and pushed through the cloud of pixie dust, moving toward the voices instead of away from them so they'd have no chance at catching the floating sparkles.

My heart leapt into my throat when Mareen and her entourage walked into view at the end of the aisle. I clutched the book to my chest, visions of this exact same thing happening to me multiple times back at school flooding my mind.

Beset by *arseholes* in one of my favorite places; another recurring nightmare brought to life.

"Hello," I said, watching the three girls as they moved to block my way out. "Doing a little reading?"

"We were going to ask you the same question," Mareen said, that soft voice of hers cutting like the sharp edge of a knife.

"I've done my reading," I said, walking up to them. "I'm actually on my way out, so if you don't mind—"

Mareen stretched her hand toward me, and I felt myself walk into a solid, invisible wall. *Magic*. Kali and Verrona giggled as I shook it off. "I'm afraid you're not going anywhere until you answer a couple of questions," she said.

"There's a guard by the door."

"Oh, I'm aware. But he won't be bothering us until we're done."

I narrowed my eyes. "I don't want trouble with you."

She brought her hand to her chest. "Nor do I. I only want answers."

"Answers to what?"

"Two questions… the first, where did you get that dress? And the second, what could the Prince have possibly wanted with the likes of you?"

"I don't know why I have to answer any of those questions."

Mareen smiled, sinister and wide. "Because you don't have a choice. If you don't answer my questions, you will be declaring yourself in open opposition to me. Once that happens, I'm afraid the gloves are off."

"I'm pretty sure the gloves were never on with you."

"They were. And so they will remain, as long as you tell me what I want to know."

I chewed the inside of my mouth, considering for a moment whether I should give them what they wanted or tell them to go and screw themselves. I knew, if I did what they asked, they would come again, and they would keep coming knowing they could strong-arm me into doing what they wanted.

If I stood up to them, though, there was no telling what they'd do to me. If the guard wasn't interested in keeping me safe, it was three against one in here; and they had magic and probably combat experience, I didn't.

At the same time... *fuck those bitches*.

"You want to know what the Prince and I talked about?" I asked. "We talked about you, Mareen. You and all the other mediocre contestants out there. And the dress? He loved the dress, because I made it myself, and because he loves the color *blue*."

Mareen frowned, and blood visibly flushed to her cheeks. "Lies," she growled. "Dirty lies!"

"Prove it."

Grunting, Mareen threw her hands toward me and sent that invisible wall crashing into my chest. I flew back several feet, staggering, falling, and landing hard on my back, the book sprawling out of my hands. I tried to get up, but a book fell on top of me, then another, and another, and another. A whole bunch of books picked themselves up off their shelves and fell on top of me like an avalanche. All the while, Kali and Verrona laughed, their voices echoing through the domed library.

I couldn't see them all walking away, but I heard their voices trailing off... replaced promptly by the sound of heavy, metal boots driving closer and closer. I was struggling to get to my feet, the weight of the books on my body making it more than a struggle for me to find my feet. But one yank of my arm was all it took for the soldier to pull me up and out of the pile and send me hurtling in the *other* direction.

This time, I managed to right myself and stop from falling down. "That hurt, you know!" I protested.

"What did you do?" he growled, his voice low, his hand reaching for the pommel of his sword.

"Me?" I shrieked. "It was them!"

"That's not what I saw."

"But it was *them*! They literally just walked away."

The soldier drew his sword. "Turn around, put your hands up, and walk," he said.

"Walk? Walk *where*?"

"Walk!"

I didn't need to be told again. I turned around, slowly, and started walking out of the library and into the adjoining hall. I kind of knew my way back to my room, but the soldier wasn't taking me to my room. He was taking me somewhere else. It didn't take long before I realized, I'd just been arrested.

Chapter Twenty

I wasn't sure what I expected a fae cell to look like. Everything about this place was so magical and luxurious, it was easy to believe even their dungeons would have the kind of amenities that would put five-star hotels to shame. This was a plain, small room, with a couch to sit on and a window overlooking the main castle domes and spires.

There was something about the way the sun hit the spires, the turrets, the domes—even the snow on the mountains in the distance—that just made everything sparkle like nothing I had ever see before. I'd never been anywhere remotely as white as this place, but even on Earth, I doubted if the snow glimmered the same way it did here.

"Are you okay?" Gullie whispered. She'd kept a low profile ever since the girls decided to bury me under a mountain of books.

"I feel like I've just been kicked in the chest by a horse," I said, keeping my voice low, "But I'll be alright."

"I wanted to beat that idiot until she started bleeding snowflakes."

"That would've been funny to watch." I kept my eye on the mountains, watching fingers of ice-cold air roll across the snow. "What do you think they're going to do to me?"

"I don't know. I doubt if anyone's ever been executed for dropping library books before, but we're talking about the fae, here."

"That's comforting, Gull." A distant flash on the horizon drew my eyes to a darkened patch of sky. Thick, dark clouds roiled beyond the mountain range. Within them, lightning bubbled in a mesmerizing way. I found myself stuck to the window, watching the clouds move and shift, watching the lightning dance inside.

Then the door opened, snapping my consciousness back into my body and into the room I was being kept in. My heart surged into my throat when I saw who had come to join me in this tiny room at the edge of the castle. Of course, it was him. Why wouldn't it be? It's not like a *Prince* would have any duties other than to come and talk to a delinquent who had made a mess in the library.

I rolled my eyes. "*Great*."

"Expecting someone else?" Prince Cillian asked, his grey-blue eyes bearing down on me.

"I guess I was kind of expecting an executioner, considering how quickly I was herded in here."

"You assume I'm not."

A shiver worked its way up my spine. "If you were…" I didn't finish the sentence, because I couldn't. If he was an executioner, *what*? He would have a sword with him? No. He didn't need a sword to deal with me. He could probably kill me with his bare hands—or teeth.

Pfft, probably. More like definitely.

"Why have I been summoned here?" he asked. His tone was neutral, flat, and cold. I didn't think he was happy about having been called to deal with whatever this was, but I also wasn't exactly thrilled at the idea that I'd been so easily thrown under the bus by those three fae. That guard had seen them come in and out, he must have, but he hadn't given me the benefit of the doubt.

Don't be stupid—the guard was in on it.

"You haven't been briefed?" I asked.

"I was briefed, but I want to hear it from you."

"Why? Just do whatever you're going to do and let me get on with this trial—unless I've been disqualified?"

He shook his head. "No. Now, tell me what happened."

"You know, I'm surprised you don't have someone else deal with this. This can't be the most important thing happening in the city today."

"Your safety and wellbeing are my responsibility."

Warm tingles invaded my stomach. "Oh..." I trailed off. "Is that so?"

"I am the Prince. You are a participant in the Royal Selection. So long as that is true, I will be summoned to personally attend to all matters involving you or any of the others. Now, no more deflecting. *What happened*?"

I frowned at him. This was another personal test, and I'd caught it before I had fallen into it. "I fell," I said.

"Fell?"

"Yes. I was reaching for a tall book, and I fell."

"You did not see the ladders scattered throughout the library?"

"Well... no, I hadn't. But the library is huge, and it's not very well organized. A person could get lost in there, never mind finding a ladder they can use to reach high up books."

The Prince's eyebrows furrowed. "Was anyone else there with you?"

"Yes, as a matter of fact. Three of the other participants."

"And did you speak to them?"

"I did. They were perfectly polite."

He paused, watching me with the intensity of a hawk. "I see. Do you know how much damage you caused with your carelessness?"

I had to bite my tongue, there. "You don't need to lecture me about the value of books... your *Highness*."

"Then how could you have allowed them to come to such needless harm?" he snarled. "Some of the books will have to be carefully and meticulously mended before they can be put into the proper place again."

Fire burned inside of my chest. I wanted to shift the blame onto the three girls that had assaulted me at the library, but I knew doing that would make me look weak. Weaker than I already was. I needed to appear strong, and there was only one way to do that. I needed to take the full blame and not flinch from it once.

"*Prince Cillian*," I said, lowering my head, "I apologize for what I did, and take full responsibility for my actions."

The Prince stared at me for a long moment, his gaze intense, his jaw tightly clenched. After a time, though, his face softened. Not much, but enough for me to notice. "Good," he said. "That was all I needed to hear."

I angled my head to the side. "I'm not being punished?"

"Do you wish to be punished, Dahlia?"

More shivers worked through me, but for different reasons. That heat burning inside of me now rushed to my face, warming my cheeks. "That's not what I meant."

"I'm sure… no, there will be no punishment to give. What has been broken can and will be fixed. However, you are not to enter the library again—not without a royal escort."

"Royal escort?"

"Though Windhelm is an incredible city in its own right, the library is my family's greatest achievement.

My father and mother were responsible for its completion and have seen to the steady addition of new titles ever since. Books from all over Arcadia and beyond sit on its shelves."

"What do you mean by *beyond?* Do you mean, from Earth?"

"Among other places…" the Prince paused, "The books we have acquired are ancient, and powerful. Some, even dangerous. There are sections of the library forbidden to the general public, not because the information within the books could be used against the Crown or our people, but because the books themselves can—and have—killed those stupid enough to attempt to read from them. After today, I would not want you to go… wandering."

Awesome. More babysitting. I frowned. The last thing I wanted was to be shadowed by this man in the one place where I thought I could get a little peace of mind. Reading was one of my comforts back home. Having the Prince hanging over my shoulder while I pored over a book wasn't exactly my idea of comforting.

It was pretty much the opposite.

"That won't be necessary," I said, "I think I've had my fair share of the library for now. I'm also not sure what the rules on checking books out is, but I doubt I'd be able to take one to my room with me."

"No. You cannot."

Nodding, I took a deep breath. I wasn't about get sent to the chopping block, and I wasn't going to be made to freeze solid in a cell. After all this, I was being let go, and that was something to be relieved by. Then I remembered what I'd read in the book, the word *Radulf* flashing in my mind like a neon sign. Not so much the word itself, but the vigor with which it had been crossed out.

"Could I ask you a question?"

"A question? Of me?"

"If I may?"

He gave me a short, polite nod. "Ask."

"Your family… I have not had the privilege of meeting his or her majesty yet, but before I do, I would like to know more about the Wolfsbanes."

"Such as?"

"Well, I didn't know they had finished building the library—which is impressive, by the way. But I suppose I also wanted to ask, do you have any siblings, perhaps?"

His eyes narrowed. "No," he said, the word cold and short. "Why do you ask?"

I looked away from him. "Oh, no reason."

"No reason?" I'd pinched a nerve. I could feel it.

"Have I offended his highness?" I asked.

"I find your behavior and your mannerisms… odd."

"That doesn't answer the question."

"It is an answer, and the only one you will get."

"Very well. Then in that case, with your permission, I would like to take my leave. Tomorrow is going to be a big day."

"It will, because tomorrow you will begin your trial at a disadvantage."

My heart hammered against my ribs. "I'm… at the bottom?"

"You are not exactly last, but yes."

I couldn't stop the question from spilling out of my lips. "*Why*?"

A pause from the Prince. "Because you have done poorly…"

"Right, but—"

"—*very* poorly—"

"—*okay*—"

"—*abysmal*, in fact. You are possibly the worst participant our city has ever seen, and with the exception of your dress, which is the only reason why you aren't at the very b—"

"—yes, *I get it*," I snapped, shutting my eyes. "I don't know why I asked the question."

The Prince opened the door. "A guard will escort you back to your room."

Breathing deeply, I walked past him and headed for the door.

"Dahlia," he called out. I hated that I liked the way he said my name. There was a growl in his voice; a low, animalistic purr that set my skin on fire. I wasn't used to feeling this way, I wasn't used to my body reacting like it did to him, and I wasn't sure whether that meant I'd lived a sad, sheltered life, or if he was just… something else.

Probably both.

I turned, slowly. "Yes?" I asked.

"Wear something white tomorrow."

"What?"

"For your trial. Wear something white. It will help you blend more easily into the snow."

I angled my head to the side, watching him curiously. Across his shoulder, the storm I had been watching earlier bubbled and shifted. "Did you just... *help* me?" I asked. "Why?"

"I am the Prince," he said, "I can do what I please, and it would please me to see you continue in this competition."

I paused. "Why?"

He stepped a little closer to me. "You are crass. You are unrefined. You are grossly underprepared for this event."

"So, it's funny to watch me flail?"

"Do you have any idea what it's like to be surrounded by people with no backbone? With yes-men and women? Nobody speaks to me the way you do. You are a refreshing change of pace, and I want to see more of you."

"Surely what that... that isn't allowed..."

He cocked an eyebrow. "Do I need to say it again?"

I swallowed hard. "You are the Prince."

"That's right. Now go, prepare. I'm eager to see what tricks you'll pull tomorrow."

The Prince opened the door to a guard, waiting to take me back to my room. I had no idea how to tell him I hadn't planned any tricks for tomorrow's trial, but now I had a clue to work with. It was time to get to work.

Chapter Twenty-One

The Prince was warming up to me, but tomorrow I faced elimination. If I was kicked out of the Royal Selection before I'd won him over, there was no telling what would happen to me. I needed to survive tomorrow's trial. Better yet, I needed to win it. The only problem was, I stood at the bottom of the pack, and that meant I was going to start at a disadvantage.

What that meant, I had no idea; but I knew one person who did.

"He said, *what*?" Mira asked.

"Wear white," I said. "Wear white, because it will help me more easily blend into the snow. What do you think it means?"

Mira shrugged. "I don't know, but if I had to guess, it's something to do with the snow."

I cocked an eyebrow. "Very clever."

She stopped pacing around the room and stared at me. "Here's the thing. Custodians are told in advance what their charges can expect in the upcoming trials, but the information we get is minimal. We know if the trial will be a physical one, a social one, a test of wits, or intelligence. That kind of thing."

"Right, that's how we were able to prepare for the last two."

"Exactly, but we aren't told what elimination trials will bring."

"So, how are contestants supposed to prepare?"

"That's just it, they aren't. Elimination trials are designed to be mysterious, all the better to test the contestant's ability to adapt to a new situation that has been sprung on them. They want it to be a surprise, so the playing field is levelled."

"If they want a level playing field, why advantage some and disadvantage others? That seems like a contradiction."

"Incentive to ensure contestants always do their best in the trials they face, I suppose."

"You mean the end goal isn't incentive enough?"

"For some, it's the competition that matters more than the prize. Even those who don't succeed, in the end, often find themselves in positions of celebrity or esteem. The more entertaining you are, the more the people will want to see of you. The Royal Selection only has one victor, but it breeds many winners."

Just like every bit of reality TV I've ever seen. It really is universal.

I looked up at her, despairing almost. "What am I supposed to do?"

Mira touched her chin with her fingertips. "The Prince giving you advice is unusual… it's possible he's trying to throw you off, so you have an even slimmer chance of winning tomorrow. But that doesn't make sense based on the interactions you've already had with him."

"So, you really do think he's trying to help?"

"I do. I couldn't tell you why… he's clearly got his own intentions, his own agenda. It may even have something to do with what the two of you talked about last night, but I can't be sure because he's obviously gone mad."

"What do you mean?"

She sighed, softly. "He called you *soulmate*. He shouldn't have done that."

I shook my head, the words *why you* rushing to the front of my mind. "But he didn't seem happy about it."

"Whatever his delusions are, all this makes me think he is trying to help you, in some way. The fact he's suggested you may have to blend into the snow makes me feel like there will be a big physical component to this trial. You'll have to hide from someone."

"Or *something*… I'm not good at fighting, Mira. The Hexquis ate my head."

"And we can't turn you into a good fighter overnight, but you're nimble, and slight. Hiding isn't out of your skillset, or at least, it's not terribly out of reach. Even for you."

"Wow… that was one hell of a backhanded compliment."

"Compliment? No. Just an observation." Mira started pacing again. "If the Prince thinks you should wear white, we should try and accommodate that."

"Do you have any idea what I'll be wearing tomorrow?"

"You won't be given anything new to wear for tomorrow's trial, which means you'll have to use the leathers you were given for your first trial. Problem is, they—"

"—are all black. Damn."

"Yes, and that stands in direct opposition to the Prince's advice."

"Can you get me another set of clothes? Something white?"

She shook her head. "I already broke rules by acquiring threads and materials for you to enhance the dress you were given the other night. Those were easier to find than a full set of working armor—especially a white set."

"So, okay… would you be able to get me more materials to work with? I can enhance the armor I already own that way."

Mira watched me intently, deep in thought. "Contestants are generally only allowed to use that which is given to them. That ensures any advantages and disadvantages handed out as part of the trial process truly mean something. But we got away with modifying the dress you were given the other night."

"Maybe no one noticed I'd altered the dress?"

Her eyebrows arched. "*Everyone* noticed. You have to understand, the royals have an innate understanding of how everyone is ranked. The moment they saw you, they knew where you stood in the rankings. They also noticed you were wearing something they had not expected you to be wearing, and yet…"

"And yet?"

She shrugged. "We weren't punished for it."

"What do you mean?"

"Well… if what you did had gone against the rules in some way, we would know about it."

I stood up from the bed and walked over to her. "Wait a second… are you telling me you aren't sure what the rules are?"

She jabbed a finger at me. "*Excuse you*, I know the rules inside and out. The problem is, I didn't expect to be given *you* as a ward. Everything is different, now. We are operating outside of established norms and traditions. That alone has destroyed every ounce of training I've absorbed over the past three years. You'll have to forgive me if I don't immediately know every answer to the strange situations we find ourselves in."

I paused, watching her eyes. "So… what can we do? What are our options?"

"I can't get you more clothes," she said. "That's out of the question."

"But materials? You've done that once before."

"And I hated doing it. Had I gotten caught—"

"—you don't know what would've happened if you'd gotten caught. Maybe something, maybe nothing. You also just said the Selection is a test of skill, right? My skill is sewing. That's literally the one thing I'm good at. Maybe it's allowed?"

She scoffed. "I hardly think I can walk around with bundles of fabric and material for you to use without attracting attention and scrutiny."

"I don't need bundles of it. I know exactly what I need, and what I need it for."

Narrowing her eyes. "You do?"

"I told you, I make magic dresses for a living, and we're in the *realm* of magic." I tapped the side of my head. "In here I keep a database of all the fabrics I've ever come across and what they do. I can give you a list of what I need."

Mira walked over to the table on which the sewing machine sat, then looked across at me. "Let's assume you're right," she said, "Let's assume they allowed the dress because it was a show of your skill. But if we're wrong, and we turn up to a trial tomorrow wearing something outlandish that isn't allowed, we'll both be in grave danger."

"So, it won't be outlandish."

"The other girls will be wearing black. You, however, will be wearing white. I think that may stand out just a bit."

I shook my head. "It won't. Look, could you trust me?"

"I want to. I really do. But there's so much on the line, here."

I nodded. "No one knows that better than I do, but if we do nothing, if we don't take the Prince's advice, I have no chance of winning tomorrow. In fact, I stand every chance of being eliminated, and if that happens, I don't know what will become of either of us."

"Well, I'll go back to my life, but you…"

"And when these glamors you're putting on me daily start to fall apart and my true nature comes out? You think I'm not going to drag your absurdly gorgeous arse down with me?"

Her eyes narrowed. "You wouldn't."

"Oh, I would. You helped a human compete. They might kill you too—or worse, destroy your reputation."

Mira frowned. "I hate you."

"Ditto, but the fact remains you need to find me things I can work with. If you do that, then I'll get us through the trial tomorrow."

"And you're sure you can do that?"

I shrugged. "No, but what choice do you have?"

A pause. "You make a valid point, but I'm still not convinced about this."

"Have I given you any reason to doubt me yet?"

Her eyebrows arched. "Yes. Plenty."

"Okay, I'll give you that, but you have to trust me now."

Mira took a deep breath in through the nose, then exhaled. "Fine," she said, on the back of a sigh. "But I want you to tell me exactly what you plan on doing with the materials you need me to get for you."

"I don't know if we have the time for that. Leather is hard to work with."

"Then make the time, because if you're plunging face-first into combat tomorrow then you're going to want to bounce your ideas off someone who has actually been in combat before."

"You have?"

"Well… no. Yes, and no. Archery is a hobby of mine… I happen to think I'm a rather good shot."

I crossed my arms in front of my chest. "And how does that translate to, *I have combat experience*, exactly?"

Mira clasped her hands together, then rapidly pulled them apart. In the growing space between them, a slender, elegant, recurve bow, emerged as if from nothing. It was black, thin, and fixed with silver trimmings and patterns; a perfect weapon for someone like her.

Before the bow could drop to the floor, Mira grabbed it firmly, notched an arrow against the string, and fired the arrow off into the wooden door to my room—all in the space of no more than three seconds. The arrow wobbled where it had struck, coming to an eventual halt.

"Holy shit…" I said. "How did you do that?"

"Let me guess," Gullie put in, "Conjuration?"

"More like summoning," Mira corrected.

"Whatever it was," I said, "That was badass. I can't do anything like that, though, and I doubt if I can sew that ability into my armor. Maybe if I was to craft some kind of pocket…"

"You won't need to summon anything, but I think I've made my point about my expertise?"

"Uh… yes, I'd say so."

"Good. So. What materials will you be requiring, and in what amounts?"

I glanced at Gullie, sitting on my shoulder. She shrugged. I looked over at Mira again. "Let me get you that list."

Chapter Twenty-Two

Today was the most important day of my life up to now.

Ever since arriving in this place, ever since my chance encounter with Prince Cillian, my life had been less than comfortable, to say the least. I had been ripped away from my home, my family, my things, and brought to a frozen wonderland where beautiful monsters played wicked games with each other's lives.

It was laughable to think that, a week ago, my biggest worry was finishing Madame Whitmore's dress on time. That my dresses were well crafted, there was no doubt. But I always struggled meeting Mother Helen's deadlines. There was always something to hold me back, if not a lack of resources to work with, then maybe the inspiration of what to do with them.

Sometimes it was just the trappings of modern life that slowed me down.

If there was one thing I had learned since getting here, one vital life lesson to take with me—assuming I would still have a life after this to live—it was this.

Procrastination was, and is, a human invention that lives only in the human world. Out here, there are no streaming services, no cellphones, no computers.

The people here lived in a way I didn't think people could live. They chased their goals with the kind of fervor humans seemed to have lost long ago, and lived every minute to improve upon the last, even though their lifetimes were far longer than a human's.

Since getting here, I had started and completed a magnificent, fitted gown in a single day. I had also modified a suit of leather armor, and packed it with hidden *surprises*, all in one afternoon. Suffice it to say, I had gotten a lot better at making sure I put every spare second of my time into my work.

"Are you ready for this?" Gullie asked as I sheathed my dagger into my belt.

I looked at myself in the mirror, then glanced at the pixie hovering near my shoulder. "No," I said, "But I have to be."

"Everything's going to be okay. The Prince helped you once already. If you win, he may help you again."

"Do you honestly think he'll send me home?"

Gullie sighed. "No. Not yet, at least. But let's focus on one thing at a time, right?"

Nodding, I examined myself one more time. The black leather armor fit me nicely, and was surprisingly more comfortable than it had been the last time I had worn it. That didn't make sense considering how I'd stuffed my face the other night. The fact that my body also looked a little more toned, a little more athletic also didn't make sense.

Turning slightly, I also realized I had an arse. An honest to the Gods *arse*. *What the hell?* A knock at the door, soft and quick. *Mira's knock*.

"Come in," I said.

Mira entered looking resplendent in a shimmering, silvery outfit. "It's time," she said, a somber look on her face.

"You don't have to look so gloomy."

She walked over to me, her eyes low, and soft. "I realized this morning… this may be the last time we are forced to tolerate each other's company."

"And that's a… sad thing? Because the words you've used make you sound relieved."

"Well, I can't say I haven't gotten… *accustomed* to your presence."

"Accustomed," I echoed, one eyebrow cocked.

Rolling her eyes, she approached. "Oh, don't be so sensitive. Humans are *so* sensitive. Now, let's fix you up before anyone realizes you're not f—"

"What?" I asked, after a pause.

She worked her fingers through my hair and lightly touched my ears. "Did I already work on you today?"

"Unless you came in while I was sleeping, this is the first time I've seen you."

Another pause. "Huh."

"Huh?"

Mira spun around me and pulled the corners of my mouth up, exposing my teeth. I swatted her away. "What are you doing, weirdo?"

"It's probably nothing… I'm just getting better at laying glamors on you."

I bared my teeth at the mirror, and sure enough, my canines were a little longer than I was used to. They were sharp, too, and pointed—like my ears. "Huh. The glamor must have lasted through the night."

Mira shook her head and laid her hands on my face. "Never mind," she said, shutting her eyes and taking a deep breath. Her magic felt like a cool breeze that made me think of the way the sunlight glimmers off the top of a frozen lake. Serene, peaceful, and immensely cold, though strangely cozy too.

"There we go," she said, examining her work. "Now you look fae."

I looked at myself in the mirror, across her shoulder. The only big change about me was the color of my hair. It was silver, now, and sparkling against the morning sunlight flooding the room. It was a strange sensation, seeing myself this way. It felt like I was wearing another person's face, and yet at the same time, I felt more like *me* than I'd ever felt.

It was weird, but I didn't have time to dwell on it.

"Alright," I said, "I'm ready."

"Are you sure?" Mira asked. "Because it's not too late."

"Late for?"

"Well… I'm sure it wouldn't look badly on me if you decided that enough was enough."

"What, you mean quit this whole thing? And do what?"

"I don't know. Maybe you could steal away and live like a commoner in the city? It might not be so bad. I was thinking about what you said about, you know, dragging me down with you, and I thought maybe I could meet you from time to time. Lay glamors on you. Maybe you could make something to wear that will make you look fae? It could work."

I stared at her, bemused. "Let's just go?"

She grabbed my shoulder. "Just… you're sure your magic is going to work?"

"Why do you ask?"

"Because…" sighing, she shook her head. "Forget I said anything. Let's go, we don't want to keep them waiting."

Nodding, I headed out of my room and down the stairs. Mira fell into step ahead of me once we reached the foot of the stairwell, where the corridors started branching out in all directions. She led me through them without missing a step, walking with confidence like she owned the castle.

Outside, a carriage was waiting to take us on a ride through the glimmering city of Windhelm. Unlike the last time I'd been out on the streets, this time I allowed myself to enjoy the view. The white walls, the spires, the domes, the way the sunlight glinted on every surface as if the city itself was frozen over.

It was magical, and fantastic. That I had ever been given a chance to see it, I realized now, was a blessing the vast majority of humans would never get. I made sure to soak it all in as the carriage rolled along streets and boulevards, all filled with fae going about their daily business of crafting, or selling their wares or their services.

Windhelm was a lot like London in that regard. Both cities bustled with activity; with trade, with commerce, with carriages. Only difference really was, this place was inhabited by otherworldly creatures, most of whom had horns on their heads and pointed ears. They looked, not quite monstrous, but definitely alien.

Although, I guess, to them, *I* was the alien.

The carriage came to a halt at a large, white gate, beyond which was what looked like an enclosed park filled with tall trees and winding paths. Several guards stood at the closed gates, waiting for us. One of the men walked over to the carriage driver to talk to him. The others watched.

"What is this place?" I asked.

"The Ancestors Glade," Mira said, "One of the most ancient sites in the city. That's where today's trial will take place."

A flash of light caught the corner of the eye and drew my attention to it. There, off in the distance and behind the mountains, dark clouds roiled and churned like angry bruise against an otherwise clear sky. It seemed closer, now. Larger. That probably wasn't a good thing, but considering no one had made a big deal of it, I decided not to worry about it.

I had bigger problems right now, like this trial.

The carriage door opened, and a slightly older, yet no less good-looking man poked his head inside. He had well-kept grey hair, pointed ears, and white antlers poking out of his temples, but it was the long, curled, grey moustache that gave him the air of sureness I detected. He looked at us both in turn, green eyes shining against the sunlight outside.

"My apologies for intruding," he said, with a deep voice I immediately recognized.

"Not at all," Mira said, "Dahlia, this is Lord Bailen—he oversees the trials contestants take."

"Wait," I said, "You're the voice."

"The voice?" he asked, puzzled.

"The announcer—you introduced the trials."

Lord Bailen gave a slight bow. "An astute observation, my dear."

"You have one hell of a voice."

"Why, thank you. You are most kind."

"Is something the matter?" Mira asked.

"I'm afraid there has been a change of plans," he said.

"Change of plans?"

"Yes, unfortunately the glade is… unavailable, for now. We will be moving today's trial to a secondary location."

"Unavailable?" I asked.

Mira gave me a harsh, wide-eyed stare that could only have meant *don't you know when to keep your mouth shut yet*?

Lord Bailen smiled. "There really is nothing to it. These things happen from time to time, but that is why we have backups." He hoisted himself into the carriage, and a moment later, it started moving.

I obviously hadn't learned when to keep my mouth shut, because I decided to ask another question. "Does the change have anything to do with the storm?"

"Storm?" Lord Bailen asked.

I cocked my thumb out the window. "That storm."

Lord Bailen leaned across me to look out at the horizon. The storm was closer, now. Closer, almost, than it had been just a few seconds ago—as if it had moved when I wasn't looking. "I shouldn't think so," he said, leaning back into his seat. "But that should make for a more interesting trial, if I do say so myself."

"Interesting isn't the right word, but sure."

Lord Bailen eyed me more quizzically, the corner of his mouth tugging into a smile. "You're her, aren't you?" he asked.

"Her?"

That slight smile turned into a full one. "The girl from the great hall, you made quite an entrance."

"Oh… *that*. Yeah, not my proudest moment."

"Pish, posh. That had to have been one of the funniest things I have ever seen."

"I'm glad to have been able to entertain."

"Oh, you did. You're quite the underdog… that will serve you well, here."

I nodded. "Good to know."

On Mira's face was a furious kind of smile. Wide-eyed, and wild; her lips pursed into a thin, stretched line. "Yes," she said, between her teeth, "Yes, it is."

Yep. Message received. If this trial didn't kill me, she would.

It wasn't long before I realized we were heading out of the city. I still couldn't recognize many of the landmarks around here, but there was one—the bridge—that even I couldn't miss. It was the long, slender neck that joined the city of Windhelm to the rest of the world.

This time, as our carriage rolled past, the people walking along the bridge would stop and wave like we were royalty.

"Why are they doing that?" I asked.

"Everybody knows about the Royal Selection," Mira said, "But not everybody can attend the festivities."

"Yeah, but why are they waving at… *me*?"

"Sweetie, I hope you haven't already forgotten what the prize for winning the Selection is? I'm sure none of these citizens would want to risk angering a potential future Queen of theirs by shunning her."

No, I hadn't forgotten that the winner of the Royal Selection was expected to marry Prince Cillian. What I had been trying to do for some time was suppress that little bit of knowledge, but Mira had helpfully brought it back up like vomit. It was hard to shake, this time. Probably because I was heading toward what could possibly be my last trial in this place.

My last trial before the truth about what I was came out.

Well, shit.

Chapter Twenty-Three

The carriage stopped at a field of frozen flowers, at the edge of a forest of snow-capped trees. Behind me, Windhelm sparkled like a crown of jewels, dominating the landscape. We were out of the city, now; away from its walls, and truly in the wild, fae country. I had been out here once before, only then I thought I was a prisoner.

Now I shared the same kind of celebrity status given to reality TV stars back home. Not only did the very notion make me feel physically sick, but the nausea only got worse as I approached the tree-line. There, the group of contestants, their custodians, and the many other fae who clearly did have the means to watch the trials unfold first-hand, was starting to look like a circus.

I disembarked from the carriage first to a round of applause by some of the *watchers* arranged behind a line of Winter Court soldiers. Mira followed me out, took my arm, and led me toward the other contestants, the applause following us all the way over. It wasn't until I reached them that I noticed Prince Cillian was here.

He was *here*.

But then, why wouldn't he be? This was probably going to be one of the most exciting trials in the entire Selection. If reality TV had taught me anything, it was that the first elimination in any such competition truly set the stage for how the rest of it was going to shape up. This was the moment where contestants made their marks, and made themselves known.

I wasn't ready for that. I didn't think I'd ever be. Collecting other people's attention wasn't exactly my strong suit, what with my social anxieties and introversion. I hated crowds, I hated being the center of attention—I even hated being adjacent to the attention. I was going to do a lot of growing up today, whether I wanted to or not.

Now was the time for me to become someone better.

"Will you please relax?" Mira asked, "You're squeezing my arm so tight I'm afraid you'll rip it off."

"Sorry…" I said, loosening my hold on her arm. "This is a bit much, isn't it?"

"It's only the beginning, and that means it will only get worse."

"Great."

Mira nodded toward the Prince. "He's watching you."

"He is?" I turned my head, dared to, and sure enough, he was watching. He wasn't smiling, or grinning. His face was stoic, and distant, but his eyes… they were as intense as ever, those blue-grey gems sparkling under his dark hair. Why did his gaze *do things* to me? More than crowds, more than attention, I hated *that* right now.

He raised his hand, made a fist with it, and immediately all the chatter and noise around me died out.

"Welcome, Courtiers," he called out, his voice booming. "We are here today to witness the first elimination trial of this Royal Selection. Before you are fifteen of the most talented, determined, and beautiful fae the land of Winter has to offer. By the end of today, there will be twelve."

"Twelve?" I hissed, "*Three* are being eliminated?"

"Hush," Mira said, "And listen."

"Lord Bailen will now explain the rules," the Prince continued, "Give him your undivided attention."

Lord Bailen, who had been standing behind me, walked past us and made his way toward the Prince's side. He scanned the girls once, then the crowd behind them, and smiled brightly. "It's a beautiful day for a trial, don't you think?" he asked, winning applause and cheers from the watchers.

Another hand gesture from the Prince shut the applause down. I got the impression he wanted to get the trial over with. Maybe the storm moving in on us had something to do with that, maybe it didn't, but the wind *had* picked up a little since I'd arrived.

"Right," Lord Bailen continued, "This trial shall be a simple one. Scattered throughout the forest behind me are a number of fairy lights that will glow as our contestants get near them. All our contestants have to do is catch them. Catch as many as you can. You will have an hour. The three with the fewest points at the end of the hour, shall be eliminated from the competition."

Sounds easy enough.

Except not really. Not when you were going up against Aronia, who looked like the kind of woman who was used to beating other people at sports. Or Mareen who, while fair and slight, probably had a ton of magic at her disposal. And that was to say nothing of the other twelve girls who had spent years training for this moment.

I was outclassed, outmatched, and worse—*disadvantaged*.

"Aronia, Mareen," Lord Bailen called out. "You will be receiving an advantage in this trial… a head start. *Go.*"

Aronia didn't need to be told twice. She shot like a bullet into the tree-line, drawing an icy blue sword as she went. Mareen gave chase, calling a handful of glowing orbs into her hand and hurling them into the forest. I couldn't see her face, but she had to have been grinning at her ingenuity. How was anyone else to distinguish her fake orbs from the real ones?

Dammit.

"The rest of you, await my signal," Lord Bailen continued.

I glanced over at Mira. "This is bad," I said.

"I know," she whispered. "Just keep calm."

"I need to figure out how to tell the real ones from the fakes. Can you help?"

"I can't interfere. If I do, and I'm caught, we're both done."

"*I can help*," Gullie said into my ear. "Get me close enough and I can tell you."

I nodded. "Thanks, Gull. Hold on, okay?"

"Always."

Lord Bailen raised his hand, named another ten contestants, and told them to go. The girls rushed into the forest in a great stampede that made the ground rumble. That left only three of us. The three most likely to be eliminated, since we were at the bottom of the pack. Luckily, the girls I was standing with looked just as nervous as I was.

Remember, you don't have to beat the leaders—only the stragglers.

I took a deep breath in through the nose, and exhaled through my mouth, shutting my eyes to help me concentrate. I wasn't sure how much time had passed exactly. Seconds? Probably more like minutes. It was totally possible Aronia had already collected the lion's share of orbs, and that was already going to make it difficult for the rest of us to find them.

That meant we wouldn't just be trying to find them; we were going to have to fight for them.

Ahead of me, I could already see many of the other contestants zipping through the forest. They looked like black splotches on the land, almost impossible to miss. I thought they would've started catching orbs by now, but instead they were fighting amongst one another, the crowd behind me roaring at the excitement of it all.

They weren't watching through the trees; they were watching proceedings through floating holographic projection that showed some of the most intense action taking place inside of the forest. It was the closest thing to live television I had seen since I got here.

The trial had barely started, and already there were at least two downed contestants. And if that wasn't bad enough, the girls next to me were eyeing me up like they couldn't wait for Lord Bailen to give the go-ahead. I hadn't used my tricks yet, I wanted to wait as long as I could before showing my hand, but if I didn't act now, these two girls had every opportunity of knocking me down before I could even make it to the trees.

Given that we were standing closest to the watchers, it looked like that was exactly what they were going to do.

It was now or never.

Lord Bailen raised his hand. I brought mine to the snowflake I had sewn into my chest. He started calling out names, and as soon as he reached mine, I tapped the snowflake, releasing the magic inside. Just as Lord

Bailen told us to *go*, the snowflake flared, a bright light catching the other girls off-guard and forcing them to shield their eyes.

I dashed away from them, heading straight for the trees, my armor transforming from black to white as I moved. This had clearly gone down well with the crowd, because now they were cheering, and clapping, and hollering; all for me.

My camouflage was working, helping me blend not only into the snow, but into the rest of the frozen wilderness around me. It wasn't just that my leather armor was now white, it was also bending the light around me, rendering me partly invisible.

"That was awesome!" Gullie shrieked. "They couldn't see us even if they weren't too busy fighting each other."

"Good, that's exactly what we want. Now, which one of these orbs are fake?"

They were everywhere, tiny balls of light zipping around the trees and between branches like frightened animals running away from predators. I tried to keep my eyes on them, but they were fast. Too fast. Catching them was going to be a challenge all on its own.

"That one," Gullie said, tugging at my hair.

I turned in the direction she wanted me to go, and sure enough, I found the orb Gullie wanted me to find. Unlike the lights Mareen had birthed, this one pulsed slowly, hovered lazily, like an deer taking a stroll through the woods. As soon as I noticed it, though, the ball of light made a sharp turn and shot in the opposite direction.

"Shit," I yelped, "I wasn't expecting it to do that!"

"What are you waiting for, then?" Gullie said, "*Run!*"

I started sprinting, following the light deeper into the forest as it tried to get away, the trees closing in a little more with every step I took. All around me, battles were taking place. Flashes of light and magic, the clash of blades, distant grunts, and shouts. Some were group fights, with three or even four girls crossing daggers to fight over a single orb floating between them. Others were skirmishes between pairs.

Neither Mareen nor Aronia were in any of these encounters. In fact, I had no idea where they were, or how far ahead of the game they had gotten. I could only concentrate on the orb I was chasing, push my body as hard as I could push it. Arms pumping, lungs burning, breaths quickening. It helped to imagine that monstrous Hexquis chasing me, its mouth slack, its wicked nails biting into the trees as it pursued its prey.

Me.

The orb dipped under a fallen log, then zipped out the other side of it. Putting my head down, I sped up as I reached it, vaulting over, and skirting across it with a kind of grace and agility I'd never known before.

It was exhilarating, I felt powerful, like a different person, but I didn't have time to celebrate, or even fully process what I had done. The little light I was chasing wasn't getting tired like I was. It wouldn't. It would keep going until long after I'd collapsed face-first into the snow.

But I had only just gotten started.

Filled with new energy, I picked up the pace, watching the orb as it skimmed past trees and over rocks and matching its every move. In moments, I wasn't only chasing it, but I was also anticipating it. Instincts guided me, instincts I'd never used before, like a muscle I'd never flexed but was ready to go at a moment's notice.

It was like a rush of adrenaline, a sudden flood of excitement. I felt like a predator, and I *liked* it.

A strong feeling in my gut told me the orb was going to make a left turn and duck behind a large rock. I decided to head straight for the rock instead of following the light. For a moment I thought it was going to suddenly circle back and go the way we'd come, but it made that left turn I had predicted it would make, and now I had it.

I took three great leaps—one onto the base of the rock, another toward the edge, and one more over it—arm outstretched, breath held in my lungs. The light slipped into my open palm, and I snagged it before it could get away.

"Gotcha!" I yelled, realizing only after that little moment of triumph that the world beneath me had started falling away.

I hadn't only leapt over a rock—I had gone over a *ridge*.

My stomach surged into my throat, butterflies dancing inside of me. I scrambled to find something to grab hold of; a branch, another rock, something. *Anything*. It was pointless. I was soaring, breathless, the ground racing up to greet me. I hit it hard against my shoulder and rolled along the snow and the dirt, smashing into rocks and outcroppings as I tumbled, flowers of pain blooming across my back, arms, and legs.

Finally, I came to a halt… face first in the snow.

Lifting my head, I spat the fluids collecting inside of my mouth, making the snow red with my blood. My mouth ached. Groaning, I pushed against the ground and hoisted myself into a seated position, then I opened my palm. The orb was still there, pulsing and glowing. I grinned, probably with a mouthful of blood, and then I remembered.

Ah, shit. Not again.

I stuffed my other hand into my hair. "Gullie?" I called out.

She wasn't there.

Panic.

My heart started thumping hard inside of my chest, my vision darkening. *She's gone. Shit. Where is she?*

"Gullie!" I yelled, my voice shooting into the woods like a shotgun blast.

A patch of snow lit up, green light radiating from within what looked like a little pixie shaped hole. Gullie pulled herself up and out, her little body soaked, her hair matted to her face. Scowling, she wiped her face with her hands, doing her best to *unstick* her hair and pull it free from her eyes.

"Well," she said, "That was a *ton* of fun."

"Look," I said, presenting the light in the palm of my hand. "We got one."

"Fantastic. I'm okay, by the way."

"Oh, calm down. I know you're fine."

Gullie shook her wings hard, struggling for a second to get airborne. She hovered over to my shoulder and sat down. "Okay…" she said, "Now, let's do that again, like ten more times. Easy."

Chapter Twenty-Four

To say that I was doing well was probably a bit of a stretch, but I'd collected three more orbs, so that was something.

When I had tumbled over a ridge earlier, I must've moved into an untouched part of the forest, because I hadn't come across another girl yet; only orbs. Orbs stuck in trees, orbs hanging around bushes, and orbs trying to bury themselves into the snow.

Still, they weren't all *legitimate* orbs, and catching them all had been one hell of a workout. I'd never moved so fast or so much in my life, and my bones and muscles made sure I knew just how upset they were with my life's choices. I had no idea of knowing whether the fae courtiers could see me all the way down here, or if maybe there was far more interesting stuff going on.

I also didn't know whether the Prince knew what I was doing or not. Given that Gullie wasn't exactly trying her hardest at keeping out of sight, I thought it was more likely that I was alone out here. If I was, then

I had the Prince to thank. I never would've thought about weaving magic into my armor, let alone magic that could better help me to blend into my surroundings.

"Up there," Gullie said, "I found another one!"

There was a little ball of light winding its way up and along the length of a tree, weaving in and out of snow-covered branches and leaves as it climbed. Above it, streaks of sunlight broke through to touch my cheeks. I shut my eyes and let the light wash over me, allowing myself a moment of rest to catch my breath.

"Is it real?" I asked.

"Yep, that's orb number five."

I moved quickly towards the tree, feeling around for decent handholds. "Ever wonder why we haven't seen any of the other girls yet?"

"I'm trying not to think about it. We may have lucked out."

"Maybe. But I can't even hear them, anymore."

"Let's just focus on the light. We already have four. That has to be enough to keep us safe from being eliminated, right?"

"I don't know. It's not like I can see a scoresheet in real time. Speaking of which, how much time do we have left?"

"Thirty minutes or so."

I turned my eyes up and took a deep breath. The tree suddenly looked a lot taller than it had a moment ago, and the orb was way up there. *Way up*. Sighing, I started climbing, using the thickest branches I could find and grabbing them close to their bases.

I was slight, but I didn't want to risk holding onto branches that couldn't support my weight. This made the climbing process slow, but I had all the time in the world, and Gullie was right. Five orbs had to be enough. All I had to do was hope it didn't suddenly decide to jump to another tree.

The next time I looked up, the sunlight was gone. The branches and snow-covered leaves were too thick to get a good look above the trees, but I didn't need to see past them to know whatever storm had been slowly making its way toward Windhelm had arrived.

The wind rushed through the area, making the branches creak and sway, and on the back of that wind I could smell… something. It was hard to tell exactly what. Maybe I was picking up the scents of this forest; many distinct aromas that individually weren't all that bad, but got all muddled up as they reached me to create something offensive.

Something sweet, and earthen, and *rotten*. It made me think of an apple fallen from a tree and left to decompose, its flesh turning black, maggots rising from within. I shook my head to chase the thought away, because I couldn't *think* it away. The image was intrusive, almost as if I hadn't conjured it at all but it had instead been put there by someone else.

"Are you alright?" Gullie asked, "Why have we stopped?"

"I'm tired," I said, taking a deep breath, "And this whole place stinks now."

"I don't like the look of those clouds. If it starts raining and we're still up here…"

"We'll freeze? I'm aware."

"I was going to say we'll probably fall and die, but freezing to a tree looks funnier in my mind, so I'll go with that imagery instead."

"You won't die. You can just fly off."

"And go where? Arcadia sucks. The fae suck. You're about the only person that cares about me. I would much prefer being dead than being stuck here without you."

"That's very sweet," I said, grunting and hoisting myself up and over another branch, "I don't have the energy to quite express how happy that makes—"

The branch snapped.

I yelped, my insides rushing toward my head as I fell. Screaming, flailing—and for the second time today—I tried to find something to grab hold of, only this time I did. I don't know how I managed to catch this new branch as I fell; some long-dormant instinct inside me must have kicked into gear. But I had stopped my fall before getting too far, only now I was dangling with one hand.

"Shit!" I yelped, "Shit, shit!"

"We're okay!" Gullie said, "We're alright. Just… breathe, and grab hold with your other hand."

Looking down made my vision swim. I pulled my eyes up and focused on the branch I was holding onto. That made things a little better. Counting to three in my head, I swung my arm up and grabbed the branch, but I wasn't near its base and it couldn't hold my weight. It, too, started to snap.

"You go," I said to Gullie, "I'm going to fall!"

"You won't, there's time. Just get to the tree."

"Easy for you to say! You don't weigh anything!"

The branch croaked as it struggled to keep its hold on its parent tree. "Go!" Gullie yelled.

I reached, one hand after the other, trying my best not to swing. I'd never done a pull-up in my life; this wasn't a skill that in my line of work was necessary. My body felt like dead weight underneath me. Still, despite the splinters biting into my hands, despite the stink, and the thoughts, and the very real threat of impending death, I moved.

One hand, then the other, then again.

But it was no use.

My insides shot up into my throat again as the branch broke and I plummeted to the ground far beneath me. I felt like I had been climbing for some time, but the fall felt somehow longer. Like I was falling in slow-motion. Despite the constant whips and snaps of branches breaking behind me, I never stopped trying to stop my fall altogether, grasping desperately at anything and nothing.

I hit the ground so hard a starfield exploded into my field of vision, the lights followed swiftly by an exquisite pain like I'd never felt before. I had landed in snow, I thought, but it felt as if I'd struck a bed of rocks. My ears were ringing, my body was a sack of pain, and no matter how much I wanted to, I couldn't move.

Somehow, I'd held onto consciousness, but I would've given anything for the world to turn black. Going under would, at least, take the pain away. And if I didn't wake up again? Well, no, that would suck. Not just for me, but also for my mothers. They would never know what had happened to me, and I couldn't live with that.

Or… die with that.

Shit, that hurts.

I tried to get up, but my muscles only screamed. I wasn't going to get back up from this. I wasn't built for this to begin with. The fact that I'd somehow managed to grab four lights was already one hell of an achievement. I had done my part, right? Now all I had to do was rest, wait for the hour to end, and get picked up by a healer.

Wrong.

Something was wrong. I couldn't see the sky from all the way under the trees, but I didn't need to. It had turned black, and sinister. The clouds weren't just moving, they were churning. Worse, the wind was churning with them, whooshing around above me.

Lightning flashed, illuminating the grove that had become my resting spot—or, possibly, my tomb.

"Gull…" I whispered; more like *croaked*, really. "Can—can you hear… me?"

No response.

I swallowed hard, pain still surging through me, pulses of agony flaring with every rapid beat of my heart. I managed to turn my hands into fists, scraping my nails through the snow, but I was far away from being able to get up. I thought I'd broken something.

I'd definitely broken something.

Maybe even something important.

Another flash of lightning, this time directly above me. I saw it tear the sky apart, the light crackling out in all directions. Strangely, thunder didn't follow the flash. It was silent, eerily silent, like an electrical storm. When You saw lightning, you expected thunder. There not being any, left me feeling weird, strange.

A third lightning strike ripped into the clouds, followed by a fourth, a fifth, and a sixth in quick succession. My heart was hammering, now, adrenaline flooding my system again to try and fight away the pain. I could move my feet, but only just.

"Gullie," I hissed, struggling with the word as the heavens threw some kind of silent tantrum.

Gullie wasn't responding, and I couldn't turn around fast enough to see where she had gone. Had she taken flight and found a branch to hang onto, or had she stayed where she was and… gotten crushed under my skull as I hit the ground?

Oh, Gods… no.

I had to dig deep, go through the pain, to find the strength to get up. I didn't care if I had to scream so loud the entire world would hear me. I got onto my side, planted my palms in the snow, and *got the hell back up*. Standing wasn't easy, my legs felt like jelly, but at least I wasn't lying down anymore.

Breathing heavily, I scanned the area for any signs of the glowing pixie.

Nothing.

The trees?

Nothing.

I called out again.

Still nothing.

Then I found her. Not because she was glowing, or flying, but because like me, she had also slammed into the snow. Only this time, she had hit it the same way I had—like a little brick. *But how?* She had wings. She could've fluttered away whenever she wanted to.

No time to question it. My stomach lurched and my heart thundered. I scrambled over to her, picked her up, and stared at her lifeless body lying in my hands.

"No…" I said, shaking my head, tears welling up in my eyes. "Gull, no… wake up." I shook her a little. "Wake up, *please*."

Her eyes were shut, her wings were a little crooked, and she wasn't moving. I also couldn't tell whether she was breathing or not. In any case, there was no way I'd be able to give her CPR. *How do you even give CPR to a pixie?* I so badly wished for a sliver of magic, anything I could use to bring her back—would've gladly given her a piece of me if it meant she would be okay—but I didn't have a way to do that.

The lightning frenzied high above, pulsing so quickly the light strobed through the forest. I stared up at it, not able to take my eyes away from the whipping, flashing arcs. One powerful bolt suddenly ripped out of the clouds and came slamming right into the ground. The earth shook beneath my feet, the world tilted, and I went down again.

The worst part wasn't the light, though, or the sound, or even the pain from the fall. It was the smell. That same sweet, mossy, rotting aroma that sent images of decaying fruit into my mind. It was maddening, having thoughts pushed into my head. Was this part of the trial? I couldn't tell, and I couldn't ask anyone, either.

When the thunder died down, all that was left was the ringing in my ears, the stench in the air, and an awful feeling in the pit of my stomach. A feeling every single human being knew all too well as soon as it surfaced. Not fear, but dread. Something had happened; something big. Maybe it was part of the trial, or maybe not, but that lightning had struck the ground not too far from me, and now the air was somehow growing impossibly colder.

Gullie coughed, weak and faint.

"You're okay!" I said, smiling at her.

Gasping, she stared at me, wild-eyed and fearful. "*Run*," she croaked, and the life fell out of her eyes once more.

Chapter Twenty-Five

Run? Run where?
Irrelevant.
I had to get up. I had to run, not because Gullie had told me to, but because I was feeling whatever she'd felt; that same urgency, that *dread*. I hadn't anticipated Gullie falling unconscious, but I *had* woven a little pouch into my armor just for her.

Carefully, I settled her inside the pouch and clipped it shut. Then I stood, adrenaline filling me, instincts flaring to life—not quite like the lioness that senses prey, but more like the deer that senses a grave threat. I scrambled to get to my feet, turned on my heel, and started running through the trees, keeping my head low and my footing as light as I could.

My body screeched with pain, each one of my muscles lending their voices to the blinding cacophony ripping through me. But I had to keep moving, keep running, get to the edge of the forest.

More and more I was starting to worry that this wasn't part of the trial. That something, somewhere, had gone horribly wrong and I was minutes away from losing my life. It was the lack of voices around me that was setting my skin on fire.

Where the hell was everyone? Where were the other contestants, where were the observing crowds, and where were the royals? It felt like they had all suddenly fallen off the face of the world, leaving me the only person in it.

No… not the only person.

I wasn't alone in the woods. There was someone else in here with me. I could feel it. Someone chasing me through the trees, silently stalking me from the shadows. There were plenty of places to hide around here. The forest was thick, the trees dense. The only thing I had going for me were my white clothes, my camouflage.

Camouflage doesn't hide the deer from the wolf's nose, though.

I had to shut my brain off. If I let myself believe that I didn't have a chance at making it to the edge of the forest, then I was already dead. I had to keep my head down and keep moving. Someone, somewhere, was bound to see me.

Then it happened.

Abruptly, I halted. I wasn't running anymore. Instead, I was rooted to the spot, my eyes wide, chest tight, my muscles stiff. I hadn't been touched, there was no one around me, but it felt like I had run into a massive, invisible cobweb I'd become stuck in. I couldn't move. My body went entirely numb, the adrenaline coursing through my veins replaced by pins and needles.

I tried to move my fingers, but it was like they were made of lead. My hands twitched, I could see my fingertips trembling from the effort, but it just wasn't working. Distantly I thought I could see someone through the gloom and the rushing wind. I tried to yell, but no words formed in my throat.

I was trapped in a living nightmare, one that was worse than every other I'd been through since I'd gotten to this wretched place.

Gull, I thought, hoping to all the Gods she'd hear me and wake up.

It didn't work.

Despite the connection we had, we didn't have a *psychic* connection; and even if we did, she'd clearly passed out again. I had to focus on moving my arms, or my legs. I didn't know why I couldn't move. It felt like the world had wrapped itself around me like a snake and was crushing my limbs, pinning them in place.

I tried to get a look at whoever was in the trees, but it was getting darker by the second save for the occasional flash of lightning from above. I could just about force the tips of my fingers to wiggle, but nothing else was working, and there was someone stalking me through the trees. Someone moving very carefully, and deliberately.

Lightning flickered above, sparkling off ice and frost and deepening the shadows between the trees. Then I caught a glimpse of turquoise from the figure moving slowly toward me, and for a moment, I thought I recognized it.

Aronia has turquoise hair.

The seconds bled into each other, turning a long string of moments into one infinitely long moment—one eternal beat of the heart. In that moment, the figure I thought was Aronia moved carefully through the forest, not like she was hunting orbs, but like she was trying to avoid detection.

But I'd already seen her. I could see her, her black, leather armor, her ice blue sword, her fair skin. It was her. Why was she skulking, and ducking, and going to such great lengths to try to avoid being noticed? Who was she hiding *from*?

The darkness moved in further, reducing Aronia to little more than a shadow with two glowing dots for eyes, and as I watched her approach, I heard something. A rustle of bushes, maybe, somewhere behind me, a snort, and then a thud. And another thud. And another thud.

The sounds vibrated inside of my chest. They made the very floor I was standing on vibrate, too. I wasn't sure what they were at first, but I wasn't waiting for long. Something moved up beside me. I felt it brush up against my arm; something big, and furry.

At first, I thought it was a bear. It certainly fit the profile. But then it moved in front of me, and I noticed it wasn't a bear. Whatever it was stood on two feet, two giant feet. This thing was huge, easily three times my size, and covered in thick, wooly, white fur. It had massive legs, and claw-tipped feet. Its arms were long and gangly; it dragged its knuckles as it walked, despite standing perfectly straight.

The giant creature stopped a few paces ahead of me, sniffed the air, and then slowly craned its head around. The sight of it made my blood freeze in my veins. Its huge mouth stretched from one side of its face to the other. It hung slack and slightly open, revealing an infinite number of jagged teeth the size of my hand.

It wasn't sniffing the air with a nose; it didn't have one. Instead, it was sucking great gulps of air through its slackened mouth, flashing its teeth every time. When it lowered its head fully to look at me, I saw its eyes. They were two dark balls inset into its almost featureless, strangely round face. From deep within them shone two tiny, almost helpless dots of white light.

When it snorted against my face, its breath hot, and heavy, the stench I'd been sensing this whole time rolled over me like a disgusting wave. It was enough to make my head spin. I almost couldn't stand it, but I also couldn't turn away. I could barely move my fingers, and now my toes. I wasn't sure what was happening.

I thought I was just paralyzed with fear. This thing was huge, and monstrous. I'd never seen anything like it, certainly not in the flesh. But I should still have been able to move. I *wanted* to move. I didn't want to just stand there and let this thing eat me, because if the spit dribbling down its lips was any indicator, this thing was hungry as all hell, and I was looking like a snack.

I hope I give you indigestion!

Another sound stole my attention, but I couldn't turn my head to find the source. It was coming from somewhere off to the right, another shuffle, another rustle—*ah shit*, another giant? No, this was lighter, somehow. Faster. A flash of turquoise leapt into the air, I caught the gleam of a blue blade, and there was Aronia, vaulting into the air like an action hero.

My heart surged, a mixture of pride and excitement filling me as the strongest competitor among us descended on this thing like a hammer. The monster stood upright and turned to face her, grunting and lazily lifting its arm up to shield its own head from Aronia's attack, but something was wrong.

The fae's sword didn't come down in a slicing arc. In fact, her eyes had gone from determined, to *terrified*. Instead of striking the beast, she *bounced* off it. I watched her slam into the giant's arm, then go spiraling to the snowy floor with a crunch. I could hear her coughing, I also thought I saw a little blood at the side of her mouth.

The giant slowly lowered its hand and turned to face the fallen fae, arching its back so as to loom over her.

Get up! I thought, screaming the words in my head. *Aronia! Get up and fight!*

But she couldn't move. She was probably in a ton of pain, but she couldn't seem to cradle her stomach, where she'd received the brunt of the impact, or even wipe the blood from the side of her mouth. And her sword? It had landed only inches from her hand, but she wasn't even trying to reach it.

All she had to do was stretch, just a little, and she'd have it; but she couldn't.

She was also paralyzed.

Now I knew there was magic at work. Something was stopping us both from moving, and it had to have something to do with this giant, this *monster*. But while she was completely paralyzed, I thought I was starting to regain a little movement in my hand. I could flex my entire palm, even though my hand was rocked by pins and needles.

I had to break free, somehow. I had to—the monster reared its head, then roared into Aronia's face. An instant later, it pulled back its arm and plunged its long, curved claws into Aronia's gut. The fae spat a glob of blood into the air that fell against her face, coloring the snow around her head a deep crimson.

I was screaming on the inside, and crying on the outside, but none of that stopped the monster from hurting her. It removed its claws from her gut, and then stuffed its own hand into its mouth. I saw its tongue stick out, long, and purple, and in a moment, it had licked the fae's blood clean off its hand, her blood now staining the fur around its mouth.

Inside of me I could feel something rising, something like anger, like fear, like desperation, all rolled into one. It was like a physical thing, a balloon I sensed that was starting to grow, and grow, filling me with warmth to fight the cold—and the paralysis. The pins and needles stretched all the way up my arms, and into my chest. I could feel them crawling up my legs, too, allowing me to wiggle my toes.

As the monster slowly dipped its claws into Aronia's open wound again, I was able—with a trembling hand—to pull my dagger out of its sheath. The fallen fae wasn't moving. Her eyes were wide open, and I could tell she was still breathing, which meant she was conscious, still alive, and likely able to feel everything that was happening to her.

My heart broke, but that only made me angrier.

With my dagger in my hand, and most of my body free from the paralysis, I chose not to hesitate any further. *This one's for Gullie*, I thought, and I surged toward the monster and drove my dagger into its shoulder. The giant groaned and turned, but it did only slowly. It wasn't quick, not of body or of mind.

I yanked my dagger out of its meaty hide, circled around it, and went to attack it again. *And this one's for*

Aronia! The dagger struck true, painting its fur with its own blood; only its blood was deep blue, instead of red.

The monster swiped at me with the back of its hand, but I was able to pull out of its path fast enough that it didn't touch me. Surprised at my own sudden burst of skill, I almost didn't react in time to its second attack. It had two hands, and the other came down on me from above. I ducked out of its path just at the last second, throwing myself into the snow to avoid getting hit.

Turning onto my back, I scrambled as the giant started advancing. I tapped the little snowflake on my armor again, sending a bright flash of light in all directions. The giant moaned and shielded its eyes, giving me ample time to get up and back away. I still had another trick up my literal sleeve, but I only had one shot at this one.

"You want me?" I yelled, "Come and get me!"

Peeling back my sleeve, I pulled a chord of carefully woven *fire-silk* until it was totally clear of my body, then I snapped it in the air like a whip, igniting the magic inside. The chord burst into flames, then exploded, sending a hail of burning embers toward the giant like they each had a mind of their own.

The monster swatted at the flames, several of them catching on its fur, others breaking almost harmlessly against it. I heard it roar and watched it flail with its long, gangly limbs, smashing them into trees to try and stop the fire from spreading throughout its body.

Then it turned to face me and roared again, its mouth falling open to reveal teeth soaked in blood, and it charged.

Chapter Twenty-Six

Instead of killing it, setting it on fire had only pissed it off, and now it was after me.

Great.

I couldn't tell whether Aronia was still alive or dead, but the fact that the monster was no longer feasting on her blood could only be a good thing. All I had to do now was concentrate on saving my own arse and hope for the best.

Despite the slow, deliberate movements I had seen this thing make until now, the fact that it had massive legs and wasn't going to be stopped by trees or branches made it very quick. I was only just able to keep ahead of it, but it was taking everything I had.

I wasn't sure where I was going. I couldn't tell which way led back to the carriage, back to the spectators, back to *safety*. Maybe if I was able to spot the city from in here, through the trees… but it was impossible to see anything beyond the forest. It was as if the very forest itself had doubled in size in the time I'd been here, and for all I knew, it had.

This was the land of magic, after all.

I felt a tickle in the back of my mind that made me look down at the pouch where I'd been keeping Gullie and saw it moving, the inside of it filled with green light. She'd regained consciousness, and she was trying to get out! I couldn't stop to fuss with the chord keeping the pouch closed, so instead I slowed, giving the monster a chance to close the distance just a little more.

It was a sacrifice, but I couldn't leave her in there — not while she could get away on her wings.

Gullie floated out of the pouch and immediately zipped into my hair. "*Alright*!" she beamed, "So! What did I miss?"

"Ice giant," I panted, "Monster, chasing, it's gross."

"What the hell is that?!" she shrieked. I guessed she'd seen it.

"Don't know. It's big, paralyzed Aronia, really hurt her." I vaulted over a fallen log and zipped behind an outcropping of rocks, putting them between me and the giant. I needed to take a break, to breathe. I wasn't going to last another ten seconds going full pelt like I was.

"This is bad," she said, "This is really bad."

"Tell me about it," I said, watching the forest for signs of movement. I couldn't hear it anymore, which meant it had also stopped. It couldn't be far, though — it had been right behind me. "Where is it?"

"I'll find out."

Gullie buzzed out of my hair and floated into the sky, leaving a trail of green light where she went. I saw her sway left, then duck right, then she came back down and landed in my hair again. "I don't know. It's gone."

"Gone? It can't be gone, it's huge!"

"Then it's worse—it's hiding."

"*Shit*."

I circled around the rocks, carefully hugging them, keeping my senses as sharp as I could. The forest around me seemed to span forever. It was dark, and full, and dense, trees everywhere, wind everywhere. It was howling, now; an animal all on its own. I was surrounded by devils and monsters, and I was all alone.

Well, not all alone.

"Can you help me find my way back to the carriage?" I asked. "It might still be there."

"I think I remember the way." Gullie said. "I'm worried about that thing, though. Where the hell is it?"

"Maybe it went back for Aronia. Oh Gods... if it went back to her, then she's dead."

A droplet of water fell on top of my head. At least, I'd thought it was water for a moment, until I realized it was warm. *Ah shit...* I didn't want to look up, I really didn't, but I turned my head up anyway, and there it was—the monster, the giant, its teethy grin endless, spit dribbling from its lips.

Spit and blood.

"Run, you idiot!" Gullie shrieked.

The monster roared and went to grab me. I had no idea how I'd managed to slide out of its hand just as it closed around my torso, but by the grace of all the Gods I'd done it, and now I was moving again, sprinting, chest heaving, lungs burning. The monster was after me again, branches snapping as it tore through them like they weren't even there.

"Where do we go?!" I yelled.

Gullie tugged on my right ear. "That way!"

Turning, and only barely managing to skirt across a patch of rock-solid ice, I kept moving, pushing blindly through the forest. Behind me, I heard a series of hard thuds followed by cracking bark. Daring to look, I stopped running and spun around on my heel to find the giant collapsed, sprawled over the patch of ice I had only just managed to make it across.

It wasn't moving.

I couldn't tell if it was breathing, but it had slammed into a huge, black tree at high speed, and at a weird angle. It had almost wrapped itself around the tree. The monster had its back to me, blue blood trickling out of and staining its fur from where I had stabbed it. I stared at it from where I stood, stuck to the spot as if I'd been frozen to it.

"Holy shit," I said. "Did we kill it?"

"I don't think we should be standing around here to find out."

"Over here!" A loud, deep voice shot through the forest, the echo bouncing between the trees.

I took a step back and threw my hands up as if *I* was the one somehow in trouble. A moment later, I heard rustling from between the trees, the crunching of boots on snow… and Prince Cillian emerged, his black hair whipping with the wind, his ice-sword drawn and ready to fight.

First, he saw the monster, lying on its side. He aimed the tip of his sword at it and moved, carefully, away from the creature like he didn't want to get too close. I didn't blame him. Despite the Prince's own impressive physique, the beast taking a nap on a small, frozen pond was at least ten feet tall. Easily the largest thing I'd ever seen.

Scanning the area, he raced toward me the moment he laid eyes on me. Gullie ducked into my hair faster than she ever had before, but the Prince had appeared so quickly, I doubted if he'd missed the soft, green glow of her wings. If he had seen her, he didn't say anything. Instead, he wrapped an arm around my waist and stared deeply into my eyes.

"Are you hurt, Dahlia?" he asked.

My lips fell open. "No," I said, "At least I think I'm okay. But Aronia, she's badly injured—she could already be dead."

"Where is she?"

I looked around, trying to figure out where in the world I had come from, but I'd almost completely lost my bearings. "I… I don't know. I can't remember which way I came, but she's in here. You have to find her!"

"The healers will find her, but we must leave this place at once."

Though I had no idea where I was, or where I'd left the other fallen fae, I couldn't bear the thought of leaving her behind. I wanted to help. I wanted to try to get her back. My staying or going could've meant the difference between her living and dying.

"I… I…" I stammered.

"Agree with him," Gullie hissed.

I nodded. "I'm glad you're here," I said, "I don't know how to get back, either."

He took my hand in his. "It's this way," he said, but he stopped moving just as quickly as he had gotten going, and I knew exactly why.

The creature was gone. The Prince had turned to take me back the way he had come. We'd taken our eyes off the giant for an instant, and it wasn't there anymore. I couldn't understand how something so large and slow could also be so stealthy. It had to have been magic of some kind—powerful magic.

"Where is it?" I asked, as my heart pounded against the sides of my temples.

He pressed his finger against his lips. "The Wenlow are adepts at remaining invisible," he whispered, "They also have the power to render their prey entirely immobile."

"It did that to me," I said, scanning the tree-line for signs of the beast.

"And you escaped?"

"I guess the spell wore off."

The Prince glared at me. "*It doesn't wear off*. How did you—?"

"I think finding the *Wenlow*, or whatever it is, should be utmost on your list of priorities, don't you think?"

The world suddenly lurched. The Wenlow had grabbed my foot and picked me up, and then I was upside down, staring into its gaping mouth. Snarling, it hoisted me up, tilted its neck toward the sky, and opened its jaws wide as if it wanted to bite my head clean off. I tried stabbing it in the arm it was using to lift me, but I couldn't reach it.

Reminder to do some sit-ups if I survive this!

A blast of magic suddenly struck the Wenlow in the chest, forcing it to stagger a few steps. Instead of letting me go, the creature pulled me closer to it, grabbing me now with both hands—one around my feet, the other around my shoulders.

If it pulled hard enough, it would tear me in two, but it wasn't interested in that. Instead, it was trying to put me between it and the Prince, whose hands were wreathed in blue fire. His eyes were glowing white, and luminous tattoos had appeared along the base of his neck, disappearing into his shirt.

"*Let her go*," he growled, flashing those large canines in his mouth.

The Wenlow held me tighter to it and roared, leaving a horrible ringing in my ears and the smell of its rancid breath lodged inside of my nose.

"I take that to mean no!" I coughed.

The Prince, who had by now sheathed his sword, curled another ball of magic into his right hand and prepared to hurl it at the beast. "I will not ask again," he threatened. "Let her go, and I will rip out your heart and put your soul to rest."

It took a minute for me to work that one out. What he'd said sounded like a threat, but the way he had said it sounded like he would be doing the creature a favor. *I'll rip out your heart and put your soul to rest?*

Still, the monster wasn't interested in what the Prince had to say. It roared again, and started pulling me apart—slowly. I screamed. I tried to wriggle out of its grasp, but the thing was way too strong. The Prince launched a ball of fire at the Wenlow, striking it on one leg and making it fall to one knee.

I fell with it, but it had to almost let me go to stick out a hand to stop its fall, giving me enough leverage to stab it in the neck with my knife. It screeched this time as a torrent of blue blood spurted from the vein I must've hit, but it still didn't let me go. This time, instead of pulling me apart, it got to its feet again and charged the prince, preparing to use *me* as a club.

The world swung around, making me dizzy. I saw the Prince prepare to duck under the attack, but his body suddenly froze, exactly the same way mine had— exactly the same way Aronia's had. This thing, the Wenlow, had successfully paralyzed the Prince of Windhelm like he was some common fae.

That was when I knew I was about to die.

My mothers flashed into my mind. Pepper, Evie, Helen. I wanted to hug them, to hold them. I wanted to sit on the blanket in our living room, sipping hot chocolate with them while Pepper read a book aloud. She loved doing that. Evie would cross-stitch while Pepper read, and Helen would sometimes crochet, or other times knit.

I would just listen.

Pepper had such a wonderful voice, so calming, and dulcet. Motherly. I couldn't count how many times she had read me to sleep as a child, and how many more times I had fallen asleep on that blanket in the living room, listening to her read. Someone would have to catch me up on what I missed the day after, but it never seemed to bother anyone.

The Wenlow swung me again, this time toward the Prince. Despite the speed at which the world tilted, I caught a flash of white in the forest, then I heard something whiz past my head and go *thunk* into the large, solid mass that currently had me in its grip.

The swing stopped half-way, the creature's hand opened, and instead of smashing into the Prince like a club, I *fell* into him like a rock, and we both tumbled through the snow. When I finally came to a halt, I turned my head up and stared at the Wenlow.

It was just standing there, swaying, with a white arrow sticking out of the side of its head.

As I watched, another arrow whizzed through the trees and struck it, then another, and another—*thunk, thunk-thunk*. They hit in quick succession, barely milliseconds apart from each other, each impact forcing the giant's head to jerk slightly. Once the fourth arrow had hit, the creature toppled slowly to the side, falling to the ground with a final thud.

The Prince groaned, and I realized then I was on top of him. I turned my eyes down and met his gaze. His black hair and beard were covered in fluffy, white snow, and he was bleeding from a slight cut on the side of his head, but his blue-grey eyes were fixed on mine.

"Sorry," I said, instantly regretting it.

Why the hell am I apologizing?

The Prince frowned. "For?"

"I… guess I bashed into you."

"That wasn't your fault… are you hurt?"

"I'm… not sure. Not too badly, I think."

His gaze deepened, intensified. Without saying anything, he reached for my face and tucked a few strands of silvery hair behind my ear, and my body responded by vibrating, entirely. His touch was electric, like a current, like cold fire. I almost couldn't take it.

"*Belore*," he whispered.

"I… I know what that means," said.

"You do?"

"I do." I paused. "Why do you keep saying that to me?"

"Because I—"

"—there you are!" Mira yelped, her voice echoing through the forest like a gunshot.

She came rushing through the trees, her gorgeous, white recurve bow in her hand. When she saw the felled Wenlow, she drew another arrow from nowhere and notched it to her bow. "Is it dead?" she asked.

"I think so," the Prince said.

I took my cue to pick myself up the moment he started squirming. The beast was dead, alright. As dead as they came. It had taken all three of us to kill it—four, if you included Aronia—but it was gone.

"What was a Wenlow doing so close to the city?" Mira asked.

"That, I do not know," the Prince said. "Get her back to the castle, I must go searching for more."

"At once, your Highness," Mira bowed, took my hand, and yanked me away.

I didn't want to go. I wanted him to finish the sentence he'd almost said a moment ago, but Mira had taught me better than to argue, and I didn't want to spend another minute in this place if I didn't have to.

Chapter Twenty-Seven

This last few days had been the most exciting and terrifying days of my life. I couldn't wrap my head around half the things I had witnessed, or experienced—which was to say nothing about half the challenges I had actually faced. The Hexquis, the constellation dress, and now the Wenlow. I mean, who the hell was I anymore?

That quiet girl who'd spend most of her days locked away in her room, sewing magic dresses, listening to audiobooks, and drinking tea, was gone; her corpse frozen solid somewhere in Arcadia. I couldn't see her when I looked at myself in the mirror anymore.

Dahlia Crowe was pasty, and dull, and a little small. But the girl looking back at me in the mirror… she stood tall, her eyes were as sharp as her canines, and her hair was the color of moondust. She was bold, scrappy, and strangely athletic.

I knew I wanted to go home, but how was I going to put this new me back in the box? Would I be able to just forget about her? The worst part was, despite everything I'd just been through, the Royal Selection had only just begun, and that meant my time in Arcadia was far from over.

How much more of this new me was going to come out during the course of the next few weeks?

"You're shaking," Mira said.

We were sitting in a waiting room somewhere in the castle, waiting to be called. I wasn't sure where. As luxuriant as the place was, with all its glittering white walls and silvery furniture, I still didn't have a feel for the place, and didn't really know where I was from one moment to the next.

I hadn't realized until she'd mentioned it, but I'd been bouncing my knee. I placed my hands on my thighs and stopped. "Sorry…"

"Don't apologize, just don't shake."

"I can't help that I don't have your icy resolve."

"Trust me, even that breaks from time to time. You've seen it."

"True…" I took a deep, shaky breath and looked around. "I hope Aronia is okay."

Mira glanced at me, her eyes narrow. "Why?"

I shrugged. "Because I saw what that thing did to her. It was vicious."

"Yes, but she's your competition. Would it not be better for our chances for her to be out of the race?"

My eyebrows arched. "Seriously? You would rather her be dead because it improves our chances?"

"I would not rather her be *dead*, only that if she is able to keep competing then that doesn't bode well for you. For us."

"I don't care about that."

"You should. It's the reason you're here."

I shook my head. "I guess compassion isn't something your people are known for, so I shouldn't expect it."

Mira paused. "No, probably not. I suppose I could try…" Another pause. "Are you… okay?"

"Is that an attempt at compassion?"

She shrugged. "I think so?"

I sighed. "Three out of ten effort, but thanks for trying. I'm alright, I'm just having trouble trying to process everything that's happened."

"Well, you did go up against a Wenlow and survive. Talking about chances, I would not have bet in your favor, let's put it that way."

"Nice." I shook my head. "What the hell was that thing?"

"Wretched creatures, really. I can't remember the last time one of them ventured so close to the city."

"Alright, but what *are* they? Was it one of those giants you talked about? The ones up north?"

"No, those are frost giants. They're different. Not as vicious as the Wenlow, but twice as intelligent *and* capable of carrot and stick styles of diplomacy. The Wenlow are… poor, lost things. Endlessly hungry. They wander Arcadia, searching for fae to consume. They are large, they are surprisingly quiet, their claws are razor sharp, and they have the power to paralyze fae they want to eat."

"I guess I saw some of that firsthand… it was licking Aronia's blood off its claws."

"And it would've eaten the rest of her if you hadn't intervened. If she's alive, it's because of you." She paused, pressing her lips into a thin line. "But I would be lying if I didn't tell you the rest."

"The rest?"

"The Wenlow are… they're the fate that awaits humans who get lost in Arcadia."

My stomach fell. "They're… human?"

Mira nodded. "It doesn't fill me with joy to have to tell you this, but it's true. Not all humans who end up lost in Arcadia become Wenlow, but under the right circumstances, if the winter chill reaches their hearts in just the right way, the transformation is inevitable. Painful, fatal, and inevitable."

"Is that why the Prince talked about its heart?"

"He mentioned that? It is said the only way to put a Wenlow out of its miserable existence is to cut out its heart and destroy it. If killed any other way, their souls are released into Arcadia where they continue to wander, lost, helpless."

I paused. "So, the one you killed…"

She nodded again. "I didn't have a choice. It was going to kill you, and maybe even the Prince."

"Is… there any way of figuring out who the person was?"

"No. Whoever they were, they stopped being that person a very long time ago. I'm only telling you this so you don't get any ideas about stealing away from the castle in the middle of the night. It wouldn't make me… *happy*… to see you succumb to such an ugly fate."

"You really had to choose your words there, didn't you?"

She rolled her eyes. "Don't make a big deal of it or I'll stop trying to reach compassion."

The large, white, double doors we'd been sitting in front of opened, and a tall, skinny man that looked like he was made of right angles stepped through. Despite being impeccably dressed in stunning, teal and silver finery, he looked about as interesting as a shelf full of encyclopedias written in a foreign language.

"The Prince," he said, exaggerating his R's, "Will see you now."

"Prince?" I asked Mira. "Is that who we were waiting for?"

She shrugged. "I'm about as lost as you are right now."

I stood, and she stood with me, but the man at the door put his hand out. "Only *she* may see his Highness."

She, meaning *me*.

Mira patted me on the shoulder. "Go. I'll wait here."

Nodding, but now suddenly infinitely more nervous than I'd been a moment ago, I walked over to the door man. He stepped aside as soon as I reached him, gesturing for me to enter a room like none I'd seen in this place yet. *This* was the kind of room my mind would've conjured up if someone had said the word ice-castle.

It was breathtaking. A vaulted ceiling, walls that shimmered white and silver, teal drapes to shield those inside from the harsh Arcadian sun. There were couches to lounge on, a table covered in exotic fruits, pitchers filled with *Clair di Lune*—that hard-hitting, Arcadian wine—and a huge bookshelf spanning almost the entire length of one wall.

There were other doors that led to other rooms and a staircase going up to another level, which gave me the impression that this was some kind of foyer; but the foyer to where?

From behind one of those doors came the Prince. He had changed since the last time I had seen him. Now he wore black pants, a frilly white shirt, unbuttoned at the collar, under a teal waistcoat. On his belt was a black sheath inside of which rested a longsword. It clinked lightly as he walked toward me, his black hair swept back, his antlers showing.

He stopped a few paces away, as if he didn't want to get too close. "Dahlia," he said.

I curtsied the way I'd seen Mira do a bunch of times. "Your Highness."

He looked like he was about to say something, but then he stopped, and he headed for the pitcher of wine and poured out two glasses. "I thought you would want to know, our healers made it to Aronia on time."

My heart surged. "Thank the Gods. I'm relieved to hear it."

"The Gods had little to do with that. Your quick thinking and courage are directly responsible for her survival."

The Prince sauntered toward me and handed over one of the wine glasses. "I wouldn't call it courage…" I trailed off. I couldn't remember the last time someone had used the word courage to describe me—or if that had ever happened at all.

"You attacked a dangerous creature without regard for your own personal safety. It was either courageous, or stupid."

"Aren't the lines between both those things blurry at best?"

The Prince arched an eyebrow. "Indeed…" he raised his glass as if to clink with mine. "To courage."

I tapped the rim of my glass with his. "To being really stupid."

He sipped. I sipped. The rush of cold was instant, flooding my throat, my chest, and trickling into my stomach. But from the cold bloomed an even stronger warmth that radiated through me with almost dizzying speed. I watched him from behind the rim of my glass, and he watched me in turn, his brilliant eyes fixed on mine.

Prince Cillian lowered his glass. "I'm curious…"

"Curious?"

"The Wenlow are known for being able to paralyze their fae prey, so they may kill and devour them at their leisure. It is a little known secret their ability works on the fae, and not other Arcadian creatures. You mentioned it had paralyzed you, as well."

"I sense a question coming."

The Prince paused. "How did you escape the paralysis?"

Because I'm not fae. "I'm not sure I know what you mean."

"It hunted you down, it paralyzed you, attacked you, and yet you broke free from its grasp—that was how you were able to attract its attention and lure it away from its meal."

I hated how he'd just referred to one of his own people, casually, as a *meal*, but I decided to let it slide. It wasn't like I had much of a choice, anyway. "How do you know all that? Were you watching?"

He shook his head. "Aronia already provided me with a full report of the events as she saw them."

"Wow… I'm impressed that she had the strength to tell you all this despite being half dead."

"Her father is the commander of the King's Guard. She is a warrior to the end. I expected no less from her." He paused. "She wished for me to offer her thanks."

I nodded. "I appreciate that, but I really don't know what to tell you. One minute I was paralyzed, and then I saw it attack her… and then I wasn't paralyzed anymore. Maybe it was adrenaline?"

"What you felt was *magic*. No amount of adrenaline would have helped you break free from its grasp."

He eyed up my leather armor. I was still wearing it. "I wonder if, perhaps, you used magic of your own."

Gingerly, he reached for the little snowflake on my chest like he was fascinated by it. Without thinking, I grabbed his hand and pulled it away, letting it go like it was red hot and burning my skin. I couldn't help it. Instinct took hold, and I broke one of the first rules Mira had ever given me.

Don't touch him.

The Prince glared at me, his eyes narrow, his nostrils flared. He looked disgusted, offended, and deeply so. "I'm sorry," I blurted. "I didn't mean to. I just—"

"—*don't* do that again," he said through gritted teeth, his voice a low, predatory growl in the back of his throat.

My entire body went cold, as if I'd been dropped in a pool of ice. "I'm sorry," I repeated. "I really am. I didn't want you to get blinded by the light."

He stared at the snowflake on my chest. "You enchanted your armor with magic. Is that how you escaped the Wenlow's grasp?"

"I… no, I already told you, I don't know how I did that. Does it matter?"

The Prince's frown steadily softened, though he looked at the hand I had touched as if he was checking for signs of injury. I couldn't understand it. The other night in his room, he had touched me. He had taken hold of my hand in the forest. He had also sniffed my hair on the streets of London. But I touch him, and suddenly he's revolted?

"I suppose it doesn't." He paused, his eyes wandering up and down my body. *Why's he doing that?*

"Is there something else his Highness wanted to speak to me about?" I ventured.

"Yes… congratulations are in order."

"Congrat—what?"

"Despite having secured the least number of orbs, your actions today have earned you your place in the next round of the competition."

"Oh… I'm not sure whether that's good or bad news."

"Why would it be bad news?"

I shrugged. "I got the fewest orbs."

"Yes, but you also got the attention of the judges."

"The judges?"

"I have no direct authority over how proceedings take place. I also could not decide who gets to stay and who must leave. That you are still here is due to the favor you have curried with them. I… would think that is a good thing."

If you even wanted to be part of this competition to begin with.

I nodded. "I guess I'll accept that, then."

The Prince paused. "There is, however, something I *can* do."

My eyes narrowed. "I'm not sure I follow."

"Aronia's family has served the crown for centuries. You saved her life… I think it would be in keeping with tradition if I were to offer you a favor in return for what you have done today."

"A favor…" I paused, "A favor from who, exactly?"

The Prince tapped his chest with his fingertips. "From me."

I swallowed hard, watching him. "And this favor… can it be anything I want?"

His eyes darkened. "That depends on what you want. Do you already have something in mind?"

"As a matter of fact, I do."

Chapter Twenty-Eight

London.

I had forgotten how loud it was, how heavy the air was, how unhappy the people looked. When all you've had for a week is the peace, quiet, and winter-crisp, clean air of a frozen wonderland, coming back to a place like this was an assault on the senses. But it was home. This was the place where I'd grown up, the place where I'd gone to school and made friends in.

And it was where my mothers were.

I had finally gotten my royal escort out of Arcadia, and all it had taken was a near-death experience with a monster. The Prince's portal opened right at the edge of the alley that led to the Magic Box, on Carnaby Street at the height of day. There were people everywhere, but nobody seemed to notice the glimmering tear in the fabric of reality or the two pointy-eared, elegantly dressed aliens stepping through it.

I dipped into the alley, if only to keep away from the hustle and bustle of the Londoners moving around the area. Turning to watch the Prince, I saw him wave a hand in front of the portal. The rings on his fingers lit up bright blue, leaving shimmering trails of light where they moved, and the portal collapsed into itself.

When he was done, he joined me a little way inside the alley itself.

"This place is…" he trailed off.

"Stinky?" I asked.

"I was going to say *quaint*."

"Oh. Yes, it's that. But it's also a little stinky. I can smell it, now."

The Prince paused, looking around the alley. "I have kept up my end of the bargain," he said, looking at me again, "Will you now tell me why you chose to use your favor on a visit to this place?"

I glanced at the Magic Box. "I want to say goodbye to the people that raised me," I said.

"And who are they?"

Turning my eyes up at him. "You really have no idea who I am, do you?"

He shook his head. "Aside from what you've told me."

"Could I ask you a question?"

"I believe you're going to ask me anyway."

"Yes, but I'm polite." I paused. "Does the Crown choose who participates in the Royal Selection?"

His eyes narrowed. "The Crown?"

"Are participants chosen based on their lineage, or their family's favor with the King and Queen?"

"No, nothing like that."

"Then, why was I chosen?"

It didn't seem like he understood what I was asking. From my vantage, it looked like he was being presented with the world's stupidest question. The kind of question everyone knows the answer to, like; *what's the queen's name*, or *who was Princess Diana?* I didn't like that look.

"Dahlia... you were chosen at birth."

My heart gave a loud *thwack* in my chest. "Birth?"

"Yes. Do you remember seeing a space for your name in the Frost Stone?"

"I... I do."

"Fate chose you for the Royal Selection long ago. Had you written a name that wasn't meant for the stone, you would not have been allowed to participate. Did your parents teach you nothing at all?"

I don't know my parents. I don't know who they are, who they were, or if they're still alive. I wanted to blurt all that out. My head was pounding with the rhythm of my heart, and my hands were starting to tremble. If I wasn't carrying a large bundle in my arms, he would've noticed. This had to be a mistake.

It had to be.

There was simply no way I was the person they thought I was. Maybe someone tampered with the stone. Maybe someone used magic to sneak me in, somehow. Or maybe fate made a mistake? How many times have tragedies occurred when they shouldn't? Fate isn't perfect. Destiny isn't always right.

It couldn't be right now.

I decided to avoid the question. "If his Highness would allow it," I said, "I'd like a moment of privacy."

Prince Cillian looked down at the door to the Magic Box, then back at me, and nodded. "Very well," he said, with a slight nod.

I turned away from him and started walking slowly toward the building. The lights in the shop were dark when they shouldn't have been. The shop should've been open at this time of the evening, but considering I had been missing for a week, I could understand why they weren't running the business.

Upstairs, though, the light to my bedroom had been turned on. In fact, as I drew a little closer to the door, I noticed a lamp had been placed on my windowpane; a lamp that shone warmly, and invitingly.

A beacon.

A wish.

A hope.

"He's not watching anymore," Gullie whispered. "Maybe we can make a run for it? Your mothers could help fight him off."

My heart soared at the suggestion. Already I could see mother Helen storming out of the shop wearing her black cloak and hat, her wand at the ready. Of all my mothers, she was my fiercest defender, and the most capable witch. If anyone had a chance against the Prince, it was her.

But I couldn't.

There was simply no way I could put her into a situation where she would have to face off against him. The risk was just too high. And if she did, somehow, kill him? At best, we bring the wrath of the winter court upon our little shop. At worst, we bring the wrath of the winter court upon our little shop.

"I can't," I whispered.

"Dee, we came all this way… this is our chance."

"It's our chance, but not to make one final stand. Haven't you been paying attention?"

A pause. "Mostly. I'm small. Lots goes over my head."

I shook my head lightly. "I can't go home. I need to see this Royal Selection thing through to the end."

"But we're *here*," she hissed. "We're *home*."

She was right. We were here. All this time I had wanted so desperately to come back home, to be reunited with my mothers. To hug them and be hugged by them. To feel safe again, to feel like *me* again. But as I reached the shop window and saw myself in its dark reflection, I knew, stepping inside wouldn't make me feel like me again.

I doubted if my mothers would even recognize me in my fae clothes, in my furry white cloak, with my silvery hair and my pointed ears. Sure, all of that would fade given time. It was only a glamor. But I knew, I would always see this version of me when I looked at myself in the mirror.

I was a beautiful stranger to the girl I had once been, and I owed it to myself to find out more about who I was. There would be no more hiding from the world after this. No matter what I did, the world would find a way to break my walls down and drag me out into it again. The best thing I could do was stare at it head on and face it, even if that meant losing my mothers.

I swallowed hard to stop tears from falling and regained my composure. "We can't stay," I said. "And I know I'm asking a lot of you… but I need your help now more than ever."

Gullie was quiet for a moment. "You've got me…" she said, her voice low. "Where you go, I go. To the end."

"To the end," I echoed.

Turning my eyes down at the bundle in my hands, I decided the best thing to do was to leave it at the doorstep. I knew, all I had to do to get my mothers' attention was touch the door, and they would know someone was down here. I wouldn't have long to make myself scarce after that, so I needed to make sure I had set everything up perfectly for them to find.

I knew I wouldn't be able to talk to them without the Prince getting suspicious, so I had decided to write them a letter and place it on top of my finest creation yet—the constellation dress. I could guarantee no one on Earth would've seen it, and with any luck, they could sell it to make their lives a little more comfortable, if that was what they wanted to do with it.

I set the roll of parchment on top of the dress, then stood, paused… and just as I was about to touch the door, I saw a face staring out at me from within the dark Magic Box.

My heart surged into my throat, and all the blood drained from my face. It was mother Evie. She looked out at me, frozen in place, her own face also turning pale. I could tell she was about to lunge toward the door, but I stuck out a hand, then I pressed a finger to my lips, and shook my head.

Evie looked confused. Her eyes were wide and white with fear, with shock. She may as well have had a sign on her forehead with the words *what the hell do I do* shining in bright, neon light.

Slowly, I backed off, letting my hand fall so as not to make the Prince suspicious. "I'm sorry," I mouthed, hoping she could see what I was saying. "I love you all."

Evie, after a moment, stepped closer to the window, then moved to the door. I turned around and started moving briskly toward the Prince, who seemed to be more interested in the passage of human foot traffic through Carnaby Street than me.

Glancing across my shoulder as I walked, I caught a glimpse of Evie picking the bundle up from the floor and unrolling the parchment in her hand. Fighting the sting of tears, I turned away from her and kept walking, not stopping once I'd reached the Prince. Instead, I made it to the end of the alley and turned out of it, disappearing from the Magic Box's view.

I didn't know what I was doing, or when I was planning on stopping, but I knew I couldn't be around when any of my mothers read the letter.

It read:

***

Dearest mothers,

I wish I had the words to tell you what's happened to me, but I'd probably need to write a whole series of books to explain it, and I'm just not that talented. Also, writing with a quill is hard.

The first thing you should know is, I'm alive, and I'm well. I promise. The second thing you should know is, I'm with the fae. I won't tell you which, and I won't tell you where, just in case you decide to try to come and find me.

Please, don't.

They've taken me to participate in some weird tradition because they think I'm someone I'm not. So far, they haven't figured out that I'm human, and I have things under control. All I know is, I have to see this through to the end. A magic voice told me so.

Anyway. I don't know when I'll be back. I just wanted you to know I'm alive. I'm okay. I miss you all loads, and I love you.

Stay strong for me, okay?

Yours,
Dahlia

Xx

p.s. I hope you like the dress. I made it myself. You might be able to fetch a few quid from those snobbish mages for it.

p.p.s. I have a pixie. Her name is Gullie. She's been with me for a long time, and I've kept her a secret from you. It felt like the right time to tell you.

***

When the Prince finally caught up to me tucked away in another, nearby alley, he looked a little alarmed. "Were you trying to flee?" he asked, "Because if so, that… wasn't a very good attempt."

I shook my head. "No," I said, hiding my tears. "We can go back, now."

The Prince placed a hand on my shoulder, another on my chin, and turned my head. "You're crying…" he said.

I swallowed. "No, I'm not."

He brushed a tear from my cheek, then held it up in front of my eyes. A moment later, it froze against his finger. "Fae don't cry."

I'm not fae.

"Could you please just take me back?" I couldn't believe I had just asked to be taken back to Arcadia. Twice.

He nodded. "Very well…" he said, his voice low. "Unless there is something else I can do for you?"

"Else?"

"All I have done is bring you here. You saved a noble's life. The scales are still unbalanced."

Pushing back the last of the tears and taking a deep breath, I glanced down the street, then stared up and into the eyes of one of the coldest fae. We were both standing so close, hidden in an alley and momentarily out of view of my world and his. I wanted to slap him once for taking me away from my home. I wanted to slap him again for being so bloody cocky.

I wanted to kiss him because my body called to his.

"There is something you could do for me…" I said, trailing off.

I thought the Prince was looming a little closer, now. "Name it," he whispered, and I could feel his warm breath against my skin.

"Lydia Whitmore," I paused. "Do you know her?"

The Prince pulled away a little and looked at me, puzzled. "I do. Why?"

"You could make sure she paid in full for the dress I made for her last week?"

A grin swept across his face, and when he smiled, he revealed his sharpened canines. "I will see what I can do," he said, and then he took a step back, and gestured toward the street.

It was time to go back. Back to Arcadia. Back to Mira, to Windhelm, and the Royal Selection. Back to that place of beautiful nightmares. Only this time, I wasn't being taken by surprise. This time, I knew where I was going and what was waiting for me.

And I was ready for it.

… to be continued.

***

Do you want more? Here's a free **BONUS SCENE** from Prince Cillian's point of view! Download it HERE!

LINK: https://dl.bookfunnel.com/hfc6apv1lt

Pre-Order book 2 right here!! And please consider leaving a review of Taken if you enjoyed it!

LINK: https://mybook.to/coldest2

***

FOLLOW ME!

Don't forget to follow me wherever you like to interact (or follow me **everywhere** so you don't miss a beat!)!

FACEBOOK GROUP

FACEBOOK PAGE

FOLLOW ME ON BOOKBUB

FOLLOW ME ON AMAZON

FOLLOW ME ON INSTAGRAM

AUTHOR'S NOTE

Thank you so much for reading *Taken*! If you're a regular reader of my books, then you know this one is something of a departure from what you're used to. I hope you enjoyed it all the same! Unlike my other series, this one draws from our real world a lot more strongly.

Dahlia, for example, works out of the Magic Shop in Carnaby Street in London. That's a real place I've been to a few times, and in fact I was inspired to write about the Magic Box during my latest trip. The Hexquis is loosely based on the Banshee, and the Wenlow is based on the real Native American myth of the Chenoo. I really wanted to ground this series into real life to try and put an emphasis on the small horror aspects that I love to incorporate into my books.

Anyway, I don't mean to keep you. I just wanted to thank you, again, for diving into this new world with me. I hope to write between 3/4 books in this series, and then write a bunch more portal fantasy romance, because I *LOVE* writing it! I hope you'll be here for the ride!

Katerina

KATERINA MARTINEZ

Also by Katerina Martinez

NEW THE COLDEST FAE
Book 1: TAKEN
Book 2: STOLEN
Book 3: MARKED
Book 4: FATED

(NEW) THE DEVIL OF HARROWGATE
Book 1: Night Hunter
Book 2: Dusk Stalker
Book 3: Dawn Strider
Book 2: Day Breaker

THE WARDBREAKER SERIES
Book 1: Heart of the Thief
Book 2: Soul of the Storm
Book 3: Crown of the Queen
Book 4: Heir to the Throne

THE OBSIDIAN ORDER SERIES
Book 1: Wings of Light
Book 2: Wings of Night
Book 3: Wings of Shadow

Magic Blood Series
The Warlock
Book 1: Demons and Deception
Book 2: Mages and Masquerades
Book 3: Scions and Sorcery
Book 4: Hellfire and Homicide
Book 5: Warlocks and Wickedness

Magic Blood Series

The Primal
Book 1: Hunter's Calling

The Blood and Magick Series

Book 1: Magick Reborn
Book 2: Demon's Kiss
Book 3: Witch's Wrath

The Half-Lich Series

THE HALF-LICH BOXED SET
Book 1: Dark Siren
Book 2: The Void Weaver
Book 3: Night and Chaos

The Amber Lee Series

THE AMBER LEE BOXED SET
Book 1: True Witch
Book 2: Dark Witch
Book 3: Shadow Witch
Book 4: Red Witch
Book 5: Devil's Witch

The Cursed and Damned Series

Book 1: The Dead Wolves

The Order of Prometheus Series
Book 1: Smoke and Shadows
Book 2: Cloak and Daggers

ABOUT THE AUTHOR

Katerina Martinez is a widely known author who writes supernatural fiction with a creepy, thrilling, and romantic bent. A veteran of many years of writing, she is the author of *Dark Siren*, the first book in the breakout *Half-Lich* Trilogy which became an instant bestseller in 2016. She continues to expand her back-list with books such as *Wings of Light*, *Heart of the Thief*, and *Night Hunter* - each a gripping addition to her already impressive roster of titles!

TAKEN

**The Coldest Fae
Book One**

Copyright © 2021 by Katerina Martinez & LJ Sampere

Visit: www.katerinamartinez.com

***

This is a work of fiction. Any resemblance to actual persons, living or dead, businesses, events or locales is purely coincidental.

Reproduction in whole or in part of this publication without express written consent is strictly prohibited. I greatly appreciate you taking the time to read my work. Please consider leaving a review wherever you bought the book, or tell your friends about this serial to help spread the word!

Thank you for supporting my work.

Printed in Great Britain
by Amazon